Books from
LILLY WILDE

A NOTE FROM LILLY

Dear Reader,

I hope you enjoy the conclusion of Branch and Ragan's story as much as, if not more than, I did. While you're here, be sure to sign up for my newsletter at http://bit.ly/2kY3dkC_ LillyWildeNews to receive FREE books from your favorite authors, up-to-date information on my latest releases, featured authors, bloggers and other interesting tidbits.

DID YOU KNOW …
This book will be available in ebook, paperback, and audiobook editions at all major online retailers!

For up-to-date information, follow me on Facebook at www.facebook.com/authorlillywilde/ or visit my website at www.lillywilde.com.

If you'd like to order a signed paperback, visit http://bit.ly/LillyWildeBooks.

REMEMBER …
When you've finished *Salvaged Hearts*, check out the snippet of my upcoming release—***Dancing In The Dark: An Untouched Series Spinoff***—included at the back of this book!

Happy Reading,
Lilly

PRAISE FOR LILLY

"This is a book like no other. These characters are under my skin, and I fall deeper with every single word."

Amazon Reviewer

"You totally killed this book! It's off-the-charts amazing!"

Goodreads Reviewer

"This story is not like anything I have ever read before—it's brilliant and amazing."

Amazon Reviewer

"I am simply not ready to leave these characters and their stories behind yet. I love this book, and I am not ready for it to be over."

Amazon Reviewer

"The conflict in these chapters is torture but wonderful. It's so amazing!

Amazon Reviewer

"This story is so damn strong…I am beyond words!"

Goodreads Reviewer

Dedication

To those whose beginnings were shattered by circumstance
but whose fighting spirit and resiliency transposed you to a
life and a love you so richly deserve.
#NeverGiveUp

Chapter ONE

Branch

"THANKS FOR HELPING ME OUT. AND MY AGENT will be in touch about those tickets," I add, shaking hands with Ragan's dad as she walks into the room.

She looks between the two of us, then settles her gaze on me, a scowl on her face. "I told you I didn't need a ride."

"And I told *you* I'd be here."

"Yeah, Ragan," David says. "It would be a big help if he drives you to work. I have a doctor's appointment this morning, so I'm going to need the car."

"You suddenly have an appointment you knew nothing about?" Ragan asks, then notices the two large cardboard boxes sitting on the floor beside her dad. "And why are my paintings out?"

"I was thinking of getting a couple of them framed for you," David replies.

Ragan squints at the stack of drawing pads, canvases, and

pieces of loose art, then returns her attention to her dad, obviously caught off guard by his response.

"You about ready?" I ask, trying to rush her out before she starts asking more questions.

Slowly pulling her gaze away from her father, she looks up at me. "I guess. But next time I say I don't need a ride—that means I don't need one. Besides, every minute you spend on me is one less you'll have for your groupies, and I'd hate to deprive those *lovely ladies* of that."

I grin and shake my head at her jab about me and Christina on the lake yesterday. When she grabs her bag, she spots the piece of paper her dad is extending toward her.

"This is for you," he says, unfolding a check. "To help with your car."

Again, Ragan appears confounded by her dad's gesture. *Why is his kindness such a shock for her?*

"I don't need—" she starts.

David shoves the check in her hand. "Don't be stubborn. Take it."

"She has that stubborn thing down to a science," I scoff.

Ragan throws me a sour look, then turns back to David. "Thanks, Dad," she says, her discomfort at extending her appreciation—and even accepting his help—obvious. She tucks the check into her purse, and her eyes drop to the drawings. "And please don't do anything with my paintings."

Ragan follows me out the door, her steps softly padding behind mine. After we've settled in the car, she looks at me.

"Do you want to say something?"

"Why were you thanking my dad?" she asks as we pull out of the driveway.

"What?"

"When I walked in…I heard you tell him *thanks*."

"Oh. A suggestion on one of my plays."

She rolls her eyes and turns to look out the window. "If you didn't want to tell me, you could have just said so. No need to lie."

"Why would I lie?"

She whips her head around to meet my gaze. "Do you seriously think my dad has pointers for *you*?"

I chuckle. "I don't know everything about football. Suggestions can come from anyone…even you, sugar."

I know she doesn't believe me, but it appears she's dropping it, which is a good thing because if she's this bothered by a ride to work, she definitely won't like the real reason I was thanking David.

"Your car will be ready around three," I say when I pull to a stop in front of the diner.

A tight smile traces her lips. "Great."

I know she's worried about the cost of her car repair, but between the tip from me and the check from David, she has more than enough to cover the bill.

"Someone from the garage will give you a call. And since I know how much you hate riding with me, someone can pick you up and get you there, too."

She opens the door and slides from the seat of the car. "Thank you…for everything. And thank Jimmy for me, too."

"No problem. Friends help friends, remember?"

"And here I thought we weren't friends, Mr. Branch," she says with an exaggerated southern drawl. "You know…on account of I'm *afraid* to be your friend."

I try not to grin as she bites her bottom lip to combat her smile. When she closes the door and heads to the diner, my eyes don't leave her. I follow the sway of her hips with each step that moves her farther away from me, suddenly realizing in spite of that smart mouth, I like Ragan. Her attitude totally pisses me off, but I definitely like her. But liking the girl I plan to fuck is never part of the equation—it's a complication.

She tosses a glance over her shoulder before stepping inside the diner, her pouty lips now pulled into a smile. For a woman who claims to dislike everything about me, her mannerisms do much to debunk that lie. Granted, she may not *want* to like an asshole like me, but I know she does. Just as I know she wants me to fuck her.

And in due time…I will.

Chapter
TWO

Ragan

"THE BLUE RIDGE BOWL IS FRIDAY. ARE YOU going?" Hayley asks.

"Nope."

"Why?"

I glance up from sorting through a stack of magazines. "Is it free?"

"Ragan, it's never free. It's a fundraising event. And tickets are only a hundred dollars this year."

"Like I said, not going. I plan to use any extra money I have toward my attorney."

"You can't live for non-pleasure alone. You need to have *some* fun."

"I can't afford a hundred dollars' worth of fun, Hayley." Unlike my best friend, I don't have parents who foot the bill for all my expenses, especially those that are strictly recreational.

"Blue Ridge High Alumni receive a fifty percent discount."

"And?"

"And I think you should go. It'll be fun. Besides, it'll give you more time to ogle Branch."

"Hmph. That guy's Jekyll and Hyde routine has given me whiplash. One day he looks at me like he wants to rip my clothes off, then he totally ignores me as he parades one of his slutty worshippers in my face the next. I've had about enough of that douche," I say and finally decide on the latest edition of *People*.

Hayley giggles. "Oh, so now he's a douche? Are you forgetting who you're speaking to? Your crush on that guy was ginormous. At one time, I thought he was your only reason for coming to school. No way is that gone."

"Well, maybe seeing him up close and personal changed my mind."

"Somehow I doubt that. Besides, you saw him up close and personal back then…remember?"

How could I forget? "How's Channing Tatum?" I ask, shifting topics.

"He's better. Not himself though."

I flip through the magazine, looking for the article about Prince Harry's wedding. At least someone gets the fairy tale. "How old is he?"

"Are you gonna start the same crap as Mom and Dad? Saying he's too old to get any better?"

I *was* thinking that, but seeing her expression makes me lie. "No. I'm just wondering how old he is."

"Oh. Well, he's only eighteen. And he'll be back to himself soon."

I don't share her affinity for the feline furballs, but even I know that's old as shit for a cat. But again, I keep my comment to myself. "I'm sure he will."

Hayley rubs her hand over her pet/friend/brother, and he somehow manages to muster enough energy to jump from the bed. I could swear I heard him grunt as he did though. Just like an old man/cat.

Chapter
THREE

Ragan

A BLOCKED NUMBER.

Answer or ignore? That's the question. Thinking it's Ethan, I tap decline and slide the phone into the back pocket of my jeans. Not even a minute later, the Halsey ringtone, *Bad at Love*, sounds again.

Another blocked call.

Definitely Ethan.

And unless he's calling to tell me this month's child support—plus the other five months he's behind—is being deposited into my account, I don't want to hear shit he says. I jab the decline icon again, only to have the ring tone sound a third time.

Figuring answering is the only way to get rid of him, I press the accept button and place the phone to my ear. "What do you want?"

"So...who peed in your Corn Flakes?"

That wasn't the voice of my ex. It's a voice I feel I should recognize though.

"Are you there?" the caller asks.

"Er…yeah. Who is this?"

He chuckles. "Man, how quickly they forget. It's Noah."

And *whoosh*, just like that, the wind is knocked from my lungs. My knees buckle, and my free hand flies to the edge of the counter, gripping it for balance. "Oh my God, Noah!"

"Now that's more of the reaction I was expecting."

"Where are you? How are you? Are you in town? Can I see you? Are you okay? Please tell me you're okay."

"Which question do you want me to answer first?"

My hand clutches my chest as I pace the length of the small space. "Stop kidding around and answer me."

"I'm good, sis. And yeah, I'm in Blue Ridge. And seeing you is one of the reasons I'm here."

What other reason would he be here? Is this really happening? Am I actually speaking to the brother I haven't seen in almost nine years? And how did he get my number?

"Have you spoken to Dad?"

"What the hell for?"

"So that's a no."

"Hell yeah, it's a no. Fuck that guy."

My mind drifts back to years past, when Dad let his bitch of a wife abuse my brother and me. And back to the day I found out Noah ran away, then to the night I confronted Dad about looking for him. I can't blame Noah for his animosity toward the father who failed us. I felt the same. I kinda still do even though I'm living under his roof. And if Noah knew I was back in the house with Dad, he'd probably hang up the phone.

"So when can I see you? I mean, you said that's why

you're here, right?"

"Yeah. I'm a few miles out, so I won't technically be in town for another half hour or so. So maybe you can meet us for dinner."

"Us? Did you bring a friend?"

"I guess you can say that."

"You guess? Either you did or you didn't."

"Yes, I did. The reason I finally came back to this shithole is because I want you to meet my fiancé."

Fiancé! "What? You're getting married?"

"It looks that way. I finally found someone who's willing to put up with me."

I try to picture a grown-up Noah—an image that would match the depth of the voice that's replaced the one I used to know. Then I try to picture a grown-up Noah with a wife. And then I try to just picture Noah. I'm unable to conjure any of those images in my head. The only Noah I can visualize is the little boy I left behind that horrible night so many years ago.

"You still there?"

"Yes," I reply, wiping at the tears that stream down my cheeks. "Just trying to catch my breath. I'm so happy for you, Noah."

"Thanks, sis."

"So what are you in the mood for? There aren't a lot of choices here."

"Is Giovanni's still on East Main?"

I hear the smile coloring his voice and I giggle. "Yes, it's still here."

"Are you thinking what I'm thinking?" Noah asks.

"Probably." Cassidy the bitch had a once-a-month girls'

night at Giovanni's. She *always* had the spaghetti and she always brought home leftovers that we could never touch. And for some *unknown* reason she always had diarrhea a couple of days after. The reason wasn't *unknown* to Noah and me. We crushed laxatives and mixed them into her forbidden-to-touch leftovers. After a few episodes, Cassidy figured Giovanni's famous spaghetti was the culprit, so she opted for a different entrée which *somehow* yielded the same result—a long night on the toilet. She and the girls finally chose a different restaurant altogether, so we stopped our food tampering, figuring she would become suspicious. Although her Giovanni's nights added to the list of things Noah and I were warned to stay away from, and although we never voiced it aloud, we both looked forward to Cassidy's Giovanni's evenings. It meant for a day—sometimes two—we didn't have to walk in fear of a beating.

I step inside Giovanni's and bypass the line of people waiting to be seated. As usual the place is packed and lively. Glasses clinking. Laughter erupting and too-loud conversation. At the hostess podium, I ask for the Prescott party. The perky blonde hostess draws a smile and then looks at her guest list.

She turns to a waitress who has the most perfect messy-bun I've ever seen and tells her where I should be directed. "Right this way," the waitress says.

I step in line behind her, a nervous smile finding its way to my lips. Nervous? Yes, nervous. I haven't seen my brother in over eight years, so I have no idea what I'm walking into or what scars he's fighting to hide. Not to mention the fiancé. He's getting freaking married!

I inhale a breath and slowly release it. I then tell myself it's just Noah. My kid brother. No reason to be nervous. I wonder if I made the right decision leaving CeeCee with Aunt Sophie. Yeah, that was probably best. I want to focus all of my attention on catching up with Noah.

As we near the table, I spot the young man that *has* to be Noah and his appearance alone stops my breath. He looks so different. His hair is not as dark anymore. And I remember it being straighter but the Noah of today has clearly channeled his inner Zayn Malik, with a curly quiff that falls naturally in the front appearing effortless and rugged. He's sporting a very light beard and a single hoop earring in one ear. He's also much taller than I imagined. He's definitely not that scrawny kid I had to worry about in the past. Noah's all grown up. And from the looks of it, he hits the gym pretty regularly—not overly buff, but those tight lines of muscle aren't exactly hiding either. *My brother is hot!* And most important, he's happy.

He stands when he sees me and the waitress says someone will be right over to take our drink order. I rush into Noah's arms and all the emotions, fears and sadness I'd carried in my heart for the last eight years buries me. The effusion of tears finally comes. I'm sobbing in his chest and when I feel his body shaking in unison with mine, I know he's crying too. I'm sure everyone in our vicinity is catching quite the show, but I couldn't care less. I finally have what I thought would remain an unanswered prayer. I have my brother.

When we curtail our emotion enough to actually look at each other, we pull back and we both fall into smiles. I cup

Noah's handsome face. His eyes, similar to the brown of mine, have a sparkle I've never seen and his once-shy smile now beams of confidence. "You look great, Noah."

"You, too, sis."

"I'm a fat ass. So stop lying."

He chuckles at my self-deprecation and we both move to sit. And that's when I notice the other person at the table. "Oh, I'm sorry. I didn't see anyone but this guy," I say, tipping my head toward my brother. You must be a friend of Noah's." I toss Noah an accusing look. "I didn't know you were bringing someone other than your fiancé. Why didn't you say?"

"I didn't say, because I didn't bring anyone else."

"I don't think I follow."

"Ragan, meet Greyson Ford, the man I intend to marry."

My head whips back to the criminally handsome man seated beside me.

#WhatTheFuck

Chapter
FOUR

Ragan

"**D**ID ANYONE EVER TELL YOU THAT IT'S impolite to stare?" Greyson asks with a charmingly playful grin that brightens the gray of his irises.

"Er…was I really doing that?" I turn toward Noah and mouth, *Oh my God.* So many things are spinning in my head right now. So, so many things. I'm finally reunited with my brother—he's literally standing inches away from me. As if that isn't already an unexpected turn of events, he's actually engaged. *To a man.* Yep, Noah's gay. And his fiancé, well he's smoking hot. I mean, come on. All of this can't be happening. Either I've stepped into some alternate universe or I'm having some type of dream with a huge subliminal message—one I will never figure out in a million years.

Greyson glances at Noah. "Looks as if she's gone from staring to stunned silence."

His voice makes my insides melt—it has that same rich

sexual depth of Chris Hemsworth's. I take a quick survey of his facial features. He has the cutest dimples I've ever seen on *any* adult and his jawline boasts the perfection of one that's been cosmetically altered. His thick mane of hair is perfectly coifed—as if he literally just hopped out of a stylist's chair. Yeah, my brother has gone off and snagged himself a super-model. Had I been in Noah's shoes, not only would I have switched teams and stepped into Greyson's lane, I would have jumped the freaking tracks just to get there! Not that Noah did anything like that, but still.

I look up at my brother whose eyes are steadfast on Greyson. And in that instant—in that single moment—I see how deeply Noah feels for this man. He adores him. Anyone in their proximity could see that—could see they make each other insanely happy. And that's what instantly fills my heart—Noah's happiness. That's all that matters.

I turn back to Greyson, embarrassed by my reaction to his modelesque looks. "I'm sorry."

He winks and flashes me a picture-perfect grin. "I was just kidding. Your reaction is pretty much in line with what Noah and I expected." Greyson pushes away from the table and pulls me into a hug.

Oh wow. He's heavily muscled…just like Noah. Not that I'm surprised seeing as how his stylishly fitted shirt molds to the contours of his physique. I literally force myself from gripping his shoulders and holding on.

Cool your loins and stop lusting over your brother's fiancé. But he's so flipping hot and it's been like a zillion lifetimes since I've had a man in my arms…or in my bed, so I tell myself that a little lusting is okay. I let go and take a few paces back and damn if his scent doesn't move with me and double-damn if he doesn't smell like panty-wetting hotness. Yeah, I know that's not an actual scent, but with this guy, that pretty much fits the bill.

"It's nice to finally meet you," Greyson says. "Noah never shuts up about his big sister."

"Jeez. Wish I could say something even close to the same. Nice to meet you, Greyson."

I look back at Noah and his eyes dart my face with that same nervous energy I had upon entering the restaurant. Clearly he's anxious about my reaction to not only a fiancé but to his sexuality. Something I never questioned to be anything other than heterosexual until now.

"Are you okay?" he asks.

I give him the smile I know he needs to see. "I'm better than okay," I say, reassuring him. "I'm perfect. *Everything's* perfect."

Noah exhales a sigh and his features visibly relax and then that beautiful smile of his reappears. We go to take our seats and as soon as we're settled, he asks, "Now that we have all of that out of the way, will you be my best woman?"

My brows rise.

"My wedding," Noah prompts for a response. "I want you to stand up for me."

I barely swallow one shock before he's hit me with another. Noah's getting married. Noah's gay. My little brother is actually in love with *a man*. And not just any man, but a man like Greyson Ford! A man that I'm practically gushing over myself. I didn't need any more time than the few minutes I'd already had to know that Noah scored big with this guy. Not that my brother hasn't transitioned into some pretty sweet eye candy himself. Good Lord, talk about a beautiful couple.

My gaze travels from Greyson to Noah, the shock of his sexual orientation still a bit unsettling. I imagine it will be for a while. Not because I'm a homophobe or anything close to it. I'd actually had a secret relationship with a girl in high school. It wasn't secret because I was uncomfortable. And I didn't really care who knew, but I only saw her when I managed to slip away from work for an hour or so. Had Cassidy found out I was having any type of enjoyment, I would've been dead. So Liberty—that was her name—was always my little secret.

I don't think in terms of gender, ethnicity or cultural differences when it comes to love—the heart wants what the heart wants. Even still, I never would have guessed this of Noah. But then again why would I have paid attention to any telltale signs back then? Our only focus was getting through the day beating-free. There was little to no time for anything but finding creative ways to please our devil-spawned stepmother.

Nevertheless, I should've known this about Noah but I didn't. Not until today. Suddenly a knot of guilt twists my stomach as I'm slapped with the reality that I suck as a sister.

"Of course I'll stand up for you," I say, reaching for his hand and giving it a squeeze. "I'm honored that you would even ask."

"Are you kidding me? Who else would I want at my side?" he asks, passing me a gleaming white smile.

"Hi, ya'll. My name is Amber and I'll be your server this evening. Can I start you folks off with something to drink?"

I turn away from Noah to see a bubbly waitress awaiting our beverage order. She's wearing a broad smile and her aura indicates she's genuinely excited to serve us. So unlike me when it comes to my customers at Jim Bob's.

Since we're celebrating a reunion *and* an engagement, I order a bottle of champagne. But before Amber heads off, Greyson asks that she bring a glass of sparkling cider for him instead. When she leaves, he explains he's an alcoholic and has been sober for the last eight years. As a matter of fact, that's how he met my brother.

Two years ago, Noah was on his way to an Adult Survivors of Child Abuse Support Group and Greyson was headed to his Alcoholics Anonymous meeting. Both groups met in the same building and one rainy afternoon, Noah and Greyson were hurrying inside and literally ran into each other. After a bout of apologies, insta-attraction and shy smiles, Greyson invited Noah for coffee after their respective meetings. And the rest is, as they say, history.

Over dinner, I watch their exchanges. The way Greyson rests his hand over Noah's when they laugh. The adorable way Noah's gaze crawls over Greyson's face as he speaks. I honestly don't think I've ever seen a couple *more* in love. Well, except Jimmy and Loretta.

Greyson tells me about his conservative upbringing and how he grew up surrounded by an amazingly supportive family who've embraced Noah with an abundance of love and enthusiasm he hadn't expected. Although Noah wasn't his first boyfriend, he was the first one he'd introduced them to. So he wasn't sure how they'd react. But it was as impossible for his family as it had been for him to *not* love everything about Noah.

Greyson turns away from me and looks at my brother. "Loving Noah was never a choice…he had me from the first moment he looked into my eyes."

Holy shit. Do men actually say things like that? I think I need a Greyson.

He pulls his gaze from Noah's and smiles at my reaction. "See what your brother does to me? One glance and I forget everything. How can I not want to spend eternity with this man?"

There he goes again. Yes, I definitely need a Greyson of my own.

"Stop it, Grey," Noah says with a grin. "You've got her all tongue-tied."

Noah calls him *Grey*. So effing hot. "Hush, Noah. I'm so *not* tongue-tied."

He looks at his fiancé and says, "Yes, she is. Look at those rosy cheeks."

"Noah, stop it," I whisper, throwing him the evil eye.

"Don't get all Cruella de Vil on me. I'm only teasing."

Grey laughs at our squabble and then goes on to share more about his alcoholism, telling me how the drinking started in high school when he was struggling with his sexuality. Coping with the stress of his family's beliefs and knowing something inside of him was in direct opposition to those teachings became a battle within a battle—conflicts he chose to fight with alcohol, which quickly shifted into a habit he couldn't break.

A near-fatal car accident with an inebriated Greyson behind the wheel forced his reality to the surface. "There's something about escaping the clutches of death that pushes one to accept his own truth. I finally admitted—to myself, at least—that I wasn't the man my parents wanted me to be. I knew I'd never be that man. And when I was fully recovered and back home, I opened up to my family about the drinking and my sexuality."

My eyes trail softly over his face. "I'm sure that must have been difficult."

"Very. I'd prepared myself for the disapproval and judgment but it never came. I never understood why because that type of admonishment fell in line with who I'd always known them to be. My guess is that nearly losing me in the accident made them realize what's most important. They embraced me for who I am—bestowing me with unwavering love and support and they made sure I got into rehab."

Noah traces a supportive hand over Greyson's as he continues his story. And then over lobster ravioli, I find myself in tears again.

"Are you okay?" Greyson asks.

"Yeah," I say, waving off his concern. "Ignore me. I'm just so full right now."

"Too much pasta?" Noah asks.

We all laugh.

"Very funny, Noah, but no. It's the two of you. You guys are what happiness looks like. And Noah, after all you've been through, it's amazing that you've found someone who can give you the unconditional love you deserve."

And that was his cue. Noah draws a breath and launches the story of his break from the Prescott household.

Chapter
FIVE

Ragan

NOAH TELLS ME ABOUT THE FAMILY WHO TOOK HIM in—the Sinclairs—and how it all started with Claudia Sinclair, a substitute teacher at Blue Ridge Middle School.

"She wasn't like the other teachers. She was attentive and kind. And it wasn't just every now and then either, it was consistent. And it was *genuine*. That was something I'd never experienced with any adult. I grew to trust her and I ultimately opened up about the house of Prescott."

Noah's face takes on a different expression. One that I know stems from the pain of the memories he fights to keep buried.

"I told her about the secret we'd been forced to keep. And I told her about you and how you'd been pushed out of our home." His eyes water and he looks up at the ceiling, drawing a deep breath. When his gaze returns to mine, he says, "I told her that with you gone, I had no one. That I was afraid for my life and that knot of fear in my gut clenched tighter every day, making it that much harder to breathe. I knew I needed to leave that house for good. Even if that meant living on the streets because that had to be safer than the lion's den I stepped into every day."

"Why didn't you come to me, Noah? You could have stayed with *me*."

Noah leans in, his gaze pressed to mine. "Ragan, there was no way you could have taken care of both of us. And as soon as Cassidy or Dad caught wind of that living arrangement, they would have destroyed it, out of spite if for no other reason."

I grab his hand, pulling it closer to me. "We would've figured something out. At least we would have been together."

"I made the best choice for both of us."

Maybe he's right. I don't know. "It was just so hard, Noah. The not knowing."

"I know," he says, his eyes full of understanding.

"What happened after you told Claudia?"

"She wanted to confront Dad and Cassidy—an idea which totally freaked me out. I told her what that would mean for me, so she backed down and made me promise I'd always let her know how I was doing. That I'd tell her before I did anything like running off. She checked on me every morning after homeroom, often surprising me with homemade treats or a new book to read. And she even helped with my studies. But all of that came to an end when she announced she was leaving Blue Ridge."

The Sinclairs were a military family and since Claudia's husband Alex was returning from his deployment, she'd be moving to Ft. Lewis. She'd waited until the day before she was scheduled to leave to break the news to Noah. She knew it would tear his heart out because she was all he had.

Unbeknownst to Claudia, the previous evening Cassidy flipped out on Noah because of an accident involving his stepsiblings. They'd been outside and Noah was watching them while Cassidy took her routine afternoon nap. As usual, the youngest wouldn't listen to Noah and tried to stand in the wagon as his sister pulled him along the sidewalk. She was going too fast, her brother lost his balance, fell and scraped his knee. When they rushed inside to get a bandage, the noise of their scrambling in the bathroom awakened Cassidy. When she asked about the incident, Noah explained what happened. She told him he should've known it was unsafe. He told her that he wasn't the one pulling the wagon, his stepsister was but she slapped him and called him a liar.

Noah grows quiet and I'm almost afraid to ask, but I do. "What happened next?"

"She said I did it on purpose and that I was turning out just like you. Then she forced me to my room. Told me to undress and assume the position."

"You don't have to—"

"I was lying there naked for about ten minutes as she beat the living shit out of me for something I didn't do. I don't know why but Dad burst into the room and told her to stop—that she'd done enough."

I remember those beatings. I remember no one ever coming to stop her either. I swipe the back of my hand over wet cheeks.

"The next day Claudia saw the bandages. The bruises. She'd overheard me telling a classmate that I'd fallen trying to mimic a skateboard stunt I'd seen on TV. But she knew that was a lie. So when she asked, I told her the truth," Noah says, shaking his head. "I remember sitting beside her desk, too embarrassed to meet her eyes. And as I sat there, reciting every detail, every rip into my skin, every cry for help… tears flowed down my cheeks. When I got to the part about Dad making Cassidy stop, I looked up and saw that Mom…I mean Claudia…was crying right along with me. She said it wouldn't happen again and that she would protect me. But I told her no one could protect me from Cassidy, which is why I'd made plans to leave that house once and for all. And that's when she said I should move to Washington with her. And without even thinking twice about it, I agreed."

Noah went on to tell me that Claudia made him aware of the implications of their decision—that no one could ever know, that he would have to forget every memory and every person in Blue Ridge. Including me. And that was the part of the plan he struggled with. He refused to leave without letting me know he was okay. So the day they left Georgia, Noah sent a message to me, telling me that he was running away. That he'd met a nice family and that he was okay. He disappeared to protect himself *and* the Sinclairs because although it was Noah's choice to leave, what Claudia had done was essentially kidnapping.

Alex and Claudia Sinclair knew right off that they wanted to adopt Noah, but they also understood the ramifications if they petitioned to do so—they'd be charged with a crime, Alex's army career would be over, Noah would get pulled into the system, or he'd end up back at Dad's. So they waited until Noah was of legal age and adopted him, making him an official Sinclair, the same as his younger sister and three brothers.

Noah has a family...a real family!

I tell Noah I want to meet the couple who saved his life... to tell them thank you. He says I can fly in whenever I want because they're anxious to meet me as well.

Breaking the darkened mood that's creeping its way through each of us, Greyson shifts the conversation to a happier topic. He tells me more about his love for Noah. About the light my brother has brought to his life, how everything that was once dark is now rich in technicolor. He speaks of their plans to have a family of their own one day and how he promises to make all of Noah's dreams a reality.

He's pretty freaking awesome. Noah did good.

"So I'm basically an open book," Greyson says. "I'm sure you have questions, so if there's anything I've left out, ask."

I glance at Noah and then turn back to his fiancé. "Well I do have one."

"Sure. What is it?"

"You mentioned having two older brothers..."

"Yeah. What about them?"

"Are either one of them as gorgeous as you, straight...*and* single?"

Chapter
SIX

Ragan

NOAH'S ONLY IN TOWN FOR TONIGHT AND tomorrow, then he and Greyson are off to Chicago to meet with a client on behalf of Greyson's father. A sense of loss creeps through me as I'm reminded that time with my brother has been reduced to hours and minutes. I try to put on a brave face, so does Noah, but it doesn't quite work. The sadness in his coffee-colored gaze is an exact replica of mine.

We go back to the hotel and talk. And talk. And talk some more. I tell him about the years we spent apart. Starting with the night Patty took me in and ending with my not-so-fabulous job. I fill him in on the adorableness of his amazing little niece. And I tell him about Ethan—down to the last detail. Noah's reaction is one of pure anger. He threatens to rip Ethan apart. After having been Noah's protector for so many years, it was surreal seeing him now in that role. And as good as it feels to know someone has my back, I make him promise to leave it alone and let me try the legal route, because that's what's best for CeeCee.

Not only is Noah happily engaged and fully integrated into his adopted family, he's a curator for one of the up and coming art galleries in Washington, and is thereby doing pretty well financially. Noah pulls out his check book and a pen. Scribbling quickly, he fills out the form, rips it from the register, places it on the table, then slides it toward me.

"Call if you need more," he says.

My gaze drops to the check, my eyes growing wide when I see the dollar amount. "Noah, this is two thousand dollars."

"I wrote it, so I know how much it is."

I make a motion to rip it in half. "I can't accept this. I won't."

Noah's hand flies to mine. "It's not for you, it's for my niece."

And then unexpectedly, tears well in my eyes. I tell him that I'm proud of the man he's become and how the hole in my heart is finally mended.

He glances at Greyson and says, "I finally have everything I've always wanted. You, Greyson, and the Sinclairs have made me whole."

I ask Noah if his sexuality was as conflicting for him as Greyson's had been. Much to my relief, Noah says that it wasn't. That he knew he was attracted to guys when he was around twelve years old. He never said anything to me or anyone else about it because he felt it would have made things that much worse for him. When he was safely tucked away in Washington, he finally voiced his truth; he told Claudia and Alex that he was gay.

Claudia surprised Noah however; she'd known for some

time and had already told Alex as much. They pulled him into the love and comfort of their home, never treated him differently, nor did he ever feel as if he didn't belong. He was finally that normal guy, with a great family. The only point of sadness had been my absence.

The pained look in his eyes tells me that our separation has been as difficult for him as it's been for me. But I'm happy he's found love and even happier that he had the Sinclairs during one of the most pivotal periods in his life. Most stories about coming out aren't as well received as his had been.

Hours pass, and with the help of coffee and sheer will, we sit and talk for hours more, until tiredness finally pulls us down. I fall asleep with Noah nestling me in his arms. And for the first time in years, I close my eyes with the knowledge that my brother is alive. That he's finally safe. And that with Greyson and the Sinclairs, he's finally home.

I awake the next morning in bed with Greyson and Noah. Noah is spooning me, and Greyson is spooning Noah. Not wanting to wake them, I slip out of bed and leave a note for my brother. On the way home, I call Aunt Sophie and ask her to stay put with CeeCee until I get there and then I call the diner and tell Jim Bob I won't be in today. A shower, fresh clothes, and a daughter later, I'm heading back to the hotel to have breakfast with Noah and Greyson.

"After the wedding, you're not gonna disappear on me again, are you?" I ask over bites of toast.

"No. That will never happen. Being away from you was hard as shit, Ragan."

We promise to always keep in touch and Noah even suggests that CeeCee and I move to Washington with him. I tell him I'll think about it, and to be honest, I'm leaning toward a yes. But there's the issue of CeeCee's relationship with Ethan. I know he'll make it next to impossible for me to leave with his daughter.

After a few failed attempts, CeeCee finally gives Noah a smile. A half hour later, she's in his lap, giggling at his silly impersonations. I snap picture after picture of the two of them and then several selfies of Noah and me.

We're soon discussing wedding dates, venues and the like when Greyson reminds us that it's time they head back to Atlanta to catch their flight.

In our final moments, Noah and I bring closure to years past.

"I hope you know I understand why you stayed away," Noah says. "I know Cassidy forced you to."

The last time I'd seen my brother was two days prior to his disappearance. He never knew, but I tell him now. That I'd always dropped by his school during recess to peek in on him. And that I'd also checked in with his teacher to make sure he was okay but when Cassidy discovered my check-ins she threatened him, so I stopped. I even tell him about my driving by the house late at night, not sure of what I was looking for but it made me feel as though I was still watching over him. And that was as far as I'd taken it. That was as far as I *could have* taken it without jeopardizing his well-being.

"I never blamed you and I never felt abandoned by you," Noah adds. "I know you were doing what you'd always done... and that's protecting me."

"Thank you, Noah." It ripped my heart out to leave him with Cassidy, but I'm glad he understands I didn't have a choice.

I choke back tears and so does Noah. I think I even see

Greyson's eyes water as he watches us. I warn Greyson to be good to my brother or I'll find him and kick his gorgeous ass. I also tell him what I'm confident he already knows—that Noah is a wonderful catch and that he deserves only the best and that I'm extremely overjoyed to know he's found that in him. Then those tears I was choking back come sliding down my cheeks. It's a sad goodbye. But this time, it will only be a short one.

Chapter
SEVEN

Branch

"I T WOULD REALLY HURT MY FEELINGS IF YOU SAY you've forgotten me," she says, a coy smile on her lips as she bats her lashes.

A resplendent contradiction—a modest seductress.

She places her palm flat to my chest, an innocent gesture to anyone who would be watching us, but I know it's everything but. "You do remember how much fun we had, don't you?"

I take a few paces back so that she's no longer touching me. And for some odd reason I *do* remember her, but I wouldn't categorize fucking her as *fun*. I wanted sex and she was eager to give it. Surely on some level she knows that's all it was. I decide not to let on that I remember her… or the sex. So I hold her gaze, not saying a word.

"It's Skye," she says, and flips her hair over her shoulder. "Skye Jamison."

Okay, so I'd forgotten her name, but that's not surprising.

But I do remember the day I couldn't get rid of her. It was last year's Annual Blue Ridge Homecoming—an event that spanned three days, the first starting with an interview with the local TV station followed by a meet and greet where I talked to fans, signed autographs and took pictures—all the normal PR stuff. Day two was the parade and day three was the game and a bonfire.

Somehow, Skye was selected to ride on the Blue Ridge High float as my homecoming queen. What a mistake that was. Afterwards, she followed me around, practically throwing her pussy at me each time our eyes met. Every chance she had to get within a few feet of me, I was met with a more suggestive proposition. Abstinence was never high on my list, so naturally, hours later I had Skye's legs slung over my shoulders as I fucked that spirit of aggression right out of her. And per my "motto", there'd been no contact since.

Judging from the way she's eyeing me, she's looking to change that, but that isn't going to happen. One night is all I want…with any woman. No one has made me want anything more. And I'm pretty damn sure that if no one has yet, no one ever will. Besides, anything in excess of a one-nighter is a one-way ticket to the bullshit that looks a lot like Mary and Curtis.

"Not interested," I say and walk past her.

She gasps at my response. "How dare you. Who do you think you are?"

I keep walking, but my steps halt at her next words.

"You arrogant bastard."

I turn on a heel and I'm face to face with her in two long strides. "What did you say?"

"You heard me."

I step closer, stopping only when I'm inches away. "What do you want? Do you want me to fuck you and then throw you aside like you're a piece of trash when I'm done? Because that's exactly what I'll do. If that's all you think you're worth, we can go at it right now, sweetheart."

I catch her hand, holding it midair just before her palm strikes my cheek. "Most women would find my offer debasing but you still can't say no, can you?"

A flicker of shame crosses her face but she quickly reapplies her veneer. "You really think you're all that, don't you?"

"Obviously *you* do."

I look up when a familiar laugh floats toward us. *Ragan.* And she looks…different. My gaze lingers on her long enough to get a rise out of Skye.

"So is that the problem? You're into fat girls now?"

"I'll tell you what I'm *not* into," I reply and drop her hand. "Aggressive women."

"You don't like aggressive. Then I won't be aggressive. I can be however you want…just tell me."

I shake my head and turn to leave.

"Branch, wait. I'm sorry for what I said. I'm not at all experienced with rejection, so maybe it bruised my ego a bit. I thought we had a great time in the past and was hoping we could have an even better one tonight but somehow we've gotten off on the wrong foot. What can I do to get us back on track?"

"You can't do anything. I'm not interested. It's as simple as that."

"You certainly were interested last year," she shoots back.

"Is that what you thought? That I was *interested*?"

"Do you fuck women that you're *not* interested in?"

33

All the time. "I'm trying to be polite."

"Where was all that politeness when you were shoving your dick down my throat?"

"Obviously you got off on it or you wouldn't be angling for a repeat."

"Do you remember what you told me?" she asks, grasping my arm before I take a single step.

I lift a brow, cueing her to continue.

"You said I sucked your dick like I was made to have it in my mouth."

No one's that special, sugar. Hell, I tell every girl that shit—as far as I'm concerned they're all made to suck my dick. She's no exception. Skye's something to look at. I'll give her that. Beautiful. Sexy. Outrageous body. And a luscious set of lips that I typically would have already pictured wrapped around my cock but the only resounding feeling I have at present is irritation. But maybe if she wasn't coming on as aggressive and desperate, I'd bend my rule and at least let her blow me again. But something about being with her a second time is fucking with my head...and my dick. I'm nowhere close to being hard, which only confirms my one-night theory.

"Just let me do that," she whispers. "I want your cock in my mouth. I want to make you come."

She's not going to give up, I can see that. I could say something harsh that would make her, but my cruelty only goes so far. And since I want to catch Ragan, and reserve Skye's mouth for some other time—just in case—I say, "Maybe later."

"I'm going to hold you to that."

Before she can say anymore, I step away, Skye and her mouth already slipping out of my mind as I head toward Ragan and her friend.

Chapter
EIGHT

Ragan

I'M IN THE BLEACHERS WHEN I SPOT BRANCH. HE'S IN loose-fitting gym shorts with compression pants underneath and a super snug matching shirt that clings to every muscle of his physique. His hat is flipped backwards and his brilliant blues are hidden behind a pair of silver-rimmed aviator sunglasses. And as typical, his presence seems to fill up the entire space around him. No doubt about it, this guy is seriously hot and completely full of himself. But who could blame him? He's by far the most attractive guy I've ever seen. When he's a few feet away, he catches me surveying that perfect body of his.

"Come talk to me."

"Why would I want to do that?"

"Because I asked you to."

"Nah, I don't think so."

He grins. "Why?"

I motion toward Hayley. "Because I can't leave my friend."

"I have friends for your friend. They can keep her occupied."

"What are you doing?" I ask. "Why are you trying to sell something I'm not interested in buying?"

"Who says that's what I'm doing? Besides, you don't know what you're passing up. How do you know you don't want to buy it?"

"Let's just say I read the reviews and I wasn't impressed."

"You sure about that? For a football game, you sure did go out of your way to get all gussied up."

"*Gussied up*? Who says stuff like that? Is that your subtle way of paying me a compliment?"

"Not really. I'm just saying you look different."

"Whatever," I grab Hayley's hand and stand to leave.

Hayley yanks her hand from mine, her lips falling into a frown. "We just sat down. What are you doing?"

I toss her a warning look. "Let's go."

"Did you do all of this for me?" Branch asks as we step past him.

I spin around to face The Kitty Whisperer. "Don't flatter yourself, playboy. I'd never waste a minute of my time on you that I wasn't being paid for."

His brows rise and his gaze falls to my chest, an area he apparently loves because I've caught his baby blues eyeing my boobs since the first day he stepped into the diner.

"You know what I mean, so get your mind out of the gutter."

His throaty laughter tickles my ears.

As usual, I sense he's poking fun. And as usual it aggravates the fuck out of me.

"How much longer do you think you can keep this up?"

"Keep what up?" I ask.

"Pretending as if I don't get under your skin."

"Oh, you do, but not in the way you think."

Of the hundreds of attendees at the Blue Ridge Bowl, Hayley and I have been "randomly selected" to participate in a game with none other than Branch McGuire. Sure, I could've said no but when it was announced that the proceeds would benefit the high school art program, I didn't want to. And now, I'm dressed in ridiculous football garb while the nation's best quarterback coaches me on how to play the game that I thought I knew all about until now.

"Hold the ball like this...with your fingers bent like so." Branch lifts the football and then rotates it three hundred and sixty degrees. "See?"

"Yeah."

"And when you throw it, don't just toss it any kind of way," he says and grins down at me. "Throw with a purpose. Have a target."

"Okay," I reply with an eye roll. Maybe I should make *him* my target. "I've got it."

"Good. And lose the attitude. We can't let a group of pre-teens kick our asses."

"But it's five of them," Hayley points out.

"I more than make up for the whole lot of 'em, but you guys have to do something," Branch reproofs.

Hayley laughs and I toss her a frustrated glance.

"Go out a few feet and let's see if Ragan can manage to get

it in your direction this time."

"Whatever," I say and grab the ball from him. I position myself to throw the ball and he stops me again.

"Spread your feet and angle back like I've shown you."

I mimic his example and he shakes his head. Stepping behind me, his hand is on my midsection and I tense. I hate that part of my body and I sure as hell don't want the likes of Branch McGuire touching it—more than likely comparing it to the abdominal muscles he's used to, those that aren't hidden by a layer of unnecessary insulation. I go to move his hand, but he resists.

"Relax, sugar," he says. His breath is warm against my ear and his foot is positioned between mine as he whispers instructions. I don't take in a damn thing he says. I'm picturing those full perfect lips and how close they are to my face. If he leans in just a couple of inches more, his mouth would be on my skin. I tell myself to zero in on his words and push the other thoughts out. But something inside my head won't cooperate. His tone is authoritative and confident, making even this simple coaching sound like a preface to a seduction…at least from where I'm standing. But I doubt he's considering anything of the sort.

I push him away. "I got it. I don't need the McGuire tutorial on how to stand."

He chuckles. "Okay. Then show me, hot stuff. Throw it."

I look down the field at Hayley. *Oh shit.*

She cups her hand around her mouth and shouts, "Come on, Ragan."

Disregarding everything Branch told me, I throw the ball to Hayley and this time it glides in her general direction just enough for her to shift right and catch it.

I look over at Branch. "See. I don't need any of your fancy football techniques. Now let's get this over with. I have an early shift tomorrow and I'm already tired."

Thanks to my disregard for Branch's advice, we lose the game, but Branch's fans and the crowd eat up every minute of the embarrassment that's the Annual Blue Ridge Bowl.

"You should learn to listen to those who are wiser than you," Branch taunts after the clock winds down.

I look up at him with a scowl. "Blow me."

"Just tell me when, sugar."

"Branch, my man. Now I *know* you aren't worth that two hundred fifty million," Matt says, coming up and shoving his friend's shoulder. "That game was an embarrassment to the sport."

Branch nods toward me. "Fault's all hers. I offered a few tips, but Ms. I-Don't-Need-Any-Help refused my advice. But I think she was trying to save face. Weren't you, Ragan?"

His eyes lock onto mine.

"You have a difficult time being close to me. Don't you?" he asks with an arrogant smirk and heads in the direction of the people standing in line to get autographs and pictures.

Matt surveys me from head to toe and then his gaze rests on mine, his lips spread into a tight sympathetic line of a smile. "Good game, guys," he lies, and follows his friend, leaving Hayley and me staring after them.

"I think Branch likes you," Hayley says, stepping up beside me.

"I think what you meant to say is, Branch likes *taunting* me."

"No, I'm serious."

"So am I. Come on, Hayley, I highly doubt he's all of a

sudden into fat chicks."

"Stop calling yourself that. You're not fat."

"Okay. Weight-challenged. Is that better?"

Hayley's lips set in a disapproving line. "Why are you always so down on yourself?"

"I'm just being realistic. Have you seen the women he dates? Well, *date* isn't the right word. I hear he gives the word *playboy* a whole new meaning."

Hayley wiggles her brows and grins at me. "So let him play with you."

I wave her off. "Just stop."

"Why should I? You were obsessed with him in high school. I mean, you would have died to have him say just one word to you. Now he's even hotter and he seems interested. Why else would he go to Jim Bob's for lunch practically *every* day? I'm telling you, there's something there. So why aren't you doing anything about it?"

Chapter
NINE

Ragan

WITH THE EMBARRASSMENT OF THE GAME behind us, I give in to Hayley's incessant whining and head back to Blue Ridge High for the bonfire. And as I scan the faces of those who didn't give me a second look in high school, I wonder what the hell I'm doing here. And furthermore, why did I think it was a good idea to play a game of Truth or Dare with this drunken bunch?

Matt looks at me with a suspicious grin spread over his lips. "Dare," he says. "I dare Branch to kiss Ragan."

I frown at Matt and shake my head. "No, thanks."

"That's not how you play Truth or Dare," Matt replies. "You can't just opt out."

I meet Branch's eyes and he winks at me. "As if you haven't already been fantasizing about my mouth on you."

"That mouth has been on half the women of Fannin County. Why the hell would I want it on me?" I retort.

"Oooh, burn." Chad guffaws.

"Kiss her, Branch," Matt says.

"Yeah, go ahead, Ragan. I dare you to let him," Hayley urges.

"Kiss. Kiss. Kiss," they all chant like a group of teenagers. All but Skye. She looks like she wants this game to end as badly as I do.

"Isn't all of this just a little too high schoolish?" I ask.

"Sure it is. We all know it, but it's tradition. This is the weekend we forget about the adulting and go back to high school," Matt says.

Branch walks over to me and reaches for my hand, then without looking up at him, I shake my head. From the corner of my eye, I catch Hayley nodding her encouragement but I still don't move. She hops out of her seat, then hurries to my side and whispers, "If for nothing else, do it to get a rise out of that bitch, Skye."

Still not totally sold on the idea, I look up at Branch and grasp his hand and he tugs me to my feet.

"It's just a kiss," he says, pulling me against his chest. His body is a thick wall of defined muscle and I'm sure there isn't an ounce of fat on him. I'm equally sure he's thinking the exact opposite about me, and my self-consciousness forces me to step back, but he cups my face and forces my eyes to his. My apprehension slips to the wayside as I gape at him, engrossed by the dancing flames flickering across his irises.

My lips part to object but the rebuttal gets lost somewhere in my head as I stare, mesmerized by that perfect mouth.

"Hey, Branch. Are you gonna make love to her or kiss her?" Chad blurts out.

The unruly group of friends becomes an assortment of

lewd prods and cackles, probably laughing at how ridiculous I look paired with a guy like Branch. But for now, I don't care.

I focus on the deliciously hot ball player; my gaze pressed to his as he leans down and brushes his lips across mine. And then he kisses me. *Branch McGuire kisses me.* He kisses me slow and he kisses me soft. He kisses me as if he has something to prove. And it's utterly breathtaking. But I sense something else, too. Something behind the dare. Something that tells me he wants a resistant sullen woman to know what she's been missing. Something that sends sparks radiating from my center and pulls me deeper into him and farther away from the onlookers situated around us.

I want to be unaffected by the kiss but it's like honey on my lips, and it touches a part of me that's never been touched. It's like every kiss I've ever had all in one—an explosion of heat that I feel in every part of me. It's everything I imagined it to be in high school, and everything I don't need it to be now. He pulls me tighter against him as he deepens our connection, his lips moving in tandem with mine with a soft, sweet tenderness I didn't expect. He prods my lips to spread and his tongue slips in, tracing the inside of my mouth with long, gentle strokes.

Something inside me shifts and my body relaxes into his. With his tongue nearing the back of my throat, he runs his hand down the line of my neck to the curve of my shoulder, then further down until he reaches my butt cheeks with a firm squeeze. Then I feel the bulge of his erection poking me in the stomach, a jab that jolts me back into self-awareness. And before I can pull away, he retracts his tongue and our kiss is over.

The previously rowdy bunch of spectators has fallen quiet.

I look up at Branch and he appears as confounded as my insides. Flustered by his intense blue gaze, my cheeks start to flush, and then he, too, is suddenly aware of his audience and his expression shifts back to the one of the cocky asshat.

"Dare completed," he says, a self-satisfied smirk spreads across his lips, then he smacks my backside as he rejoins the others around the fire.

Behind me, the fellas cajole Branch about being smitten. I turn to face the group, my eyes dart to Hayley who's bouncing in her seat with a silly grin and two thumbs up. Then I look at Skye who appears as though she wants to scratch my eyes out. Her reaction alone was worth being on display for Branch's friends. And then I evaluate my own response—my heart racing, my panties insta-wet and my lips burning from the heat of his touch.

As if nothing out of the ordinary has happened—and it probably hasn't for them—everything falls back to normal. Conversations commence, laughter floats through the night air and beer bottles clink. Chad passes me a fresh one when he sees my hand is empty. He taps the neck of his with mine and then takes a seat between Hayley and me. "I think we should take this party to the cabin," he suggests.

"I'm game," Matt says.

"What cabin?" I ask as Darcy rejoins our ever-growing circle.

"My parents'. We always go there when Branch honors us with his annual homecoming," she says, flashing a smile in his direction. "It's become somewhat of a tradition, I guess."

"Yeah, let's do it," Todd agrees.

I look around as everyone starts gathering their things. I have no idea how I've been pulled into the popular crowd that shunned me in high school.

I'm on my third beer. Maybe fourth. Quite frankly, I've lost count. But since I'm seeing two of everything and the room is spinning, I'm sure I've surpassed my limit. The space is partially lit by the tall lamp in the far corner; the fire crackling a few feet away from me is the only other source of illumination. I make my way to the sofa and fall onto Hayley. She nudges me to look at the figures on the opposite side of the room. At first glance, it's four of them, but after some serious squinting, I see it's only two. Skye has somehow maneuvered her way into Branch's arms and she's taking full advantage of the opportunity. Her body is practically glued to his, every curve of her body is touching the muscled contours of his. And here I am, sitting on the sidelines, half-drunk, watching the popular couple, the whole time wishing it was me…just like in high school. The difference now is that I'm apparently one of them, which means I don't have to sit by and watch. I should be the one in his arms but I know that is just as unlikely now as it was then. I frown in their direction. I swear if he wanted to screw her right here in front of us, she'd be all for it. When Todd joins them, Branch disentangles himself and goes to the kitchen.

"Now's your chance," Hayley says.

"For what?"

"Must I state the obvious?"

"I'm guessing you do because I don't know what the hell you're talking about."

Branch reenters the room with a bottle of water in one hand and a beer in the other.

"How about another round of Truth or Dare?" Hayley asks.

"Yeah, but let's up the stakes," Chad says, pouncing on the sofa beside us.

"I say we finish what Branch and Ragan started," Hayley suggests, a sly smile on her lips.

I look at Branch and my insides tighten as I recall the kiss at the bonfire. He lifts the bottle to his lips, takes a sip and then winks at me.

Matt finishes off his drink and places the empty container on the table. "Everyone in?"

Even before we confirm, he spins the bottle. When it stops, the neck is pointed to Skye. "Okay, I'm first. This one is for you, Skye," Matt says. "Truth or Dare."

"Truth," Skye replies.

"You only came with us tonight in hopes of scoring with Branch."

She looks at me, then at Branch, and smiles. "No offense to anyone here, but yes. It's true."

My gaze flashes back to Branch and he appears unaffected by Skye's admission.

Skye takes a turn spinning the bottle and it points to Hayley. "Truth or Dare."

"Truth," Hayley replies.

"How often do you masturbate?"

I look at Hayley and she scoffs. If Skye was hoping to embarrass someone, she picked the wrong girl.

"A lot," Hayley replies and grabs the bottle. After her spin, it's pointing toward Branch. "Truth or Dare," she says.

He swallows the last of his beer and says, "Dare."

"I dare you to have sex with Ragan," Hayley blurts out.

"What the hell?" I elbow her.

"What? We're all adults. You can say no. So can he. Jeez."

"Why is everyone so focused on Branch and Ragan? They are clearly not a match," Skye says with a discerning air, as if she's imparting wisdom.

"Good thing this is Truth or Dare and not Matchmaker," Hayley replies.

The guys egg Branch on and I sit in drunken silence. Yes, this is feeling more and more like high school with each passing minute.

Branch looks at me. I can't tell if he's okay with what he's seeing or not because he gives nothing away. "I'm game if you are."

"You've got to be kidding me," Skye scoffs.

"Mind your own freaking business," Hayley retorts to the uppity blonde.

"As if anyone is talking to you," Skye replies.

"I haven't seen a girl fight since our senior trip to Panama City Beach, and these two are way hotter so this should be good," Matt says, rubbing his hands over each other as though he's just uncovered a sinister plot.

Ignoring the impending squabble sounding around me, my eyes remain fixed on the hottest guy in the cabin, wondering if he's for real and then just like at the bonfire, he stands and holds a hand out to me. And just like then, I hesitate.

"Where's all that sass and attitude now?" Branch asks.

The egging on and near-fight jabs fall into silence as everyone awaits my response. My breaths come shorter and my heart is thumping to some weird erratic beat.

In the next second, Hayley is in my ear. "Told you he likes you. Do it, Ragan. You will definitely regret it if you don't."

I shrug her away and with my gaze pinned to Branch, and my heart still trying to escape my chest, I stand and place my hand in his. Then finally, I reply, "If you don't think you're too wasted to get it up, let's do it."

"Ah, there she is," he says and curves his fingers over my hand and tugs me behind him.

As the guys whistle and applaud like the childish men they are, I toss a nervous glance over my shoulder at Hayley. She's nodding her approval with those damn two thumbs up again.

Branch's hand squeezes mine as he leads me up the stairs and with each step my anxiety increases. *What the hell am I doing? This is crazy. Responsible adults don't do shit like this.* But isn't that the point of everything tonight? To forgo the responsibilities of our everyday lives and do something wild and crazy?

When we reach the second door on the top floor, Branch pushes it open, moves to the side and, gestures for me to step into the bedroom.

I swallow the bundle of nerves and cross the threshold.

Once he's closed and locked the door behind him, he steps in front of me and leans down, and with his lips touching my earlobe, he whispers, "Finally."

The warmth of his breath and the barely there touch of his mouth sends a trail of gooseflesh over my skin.

He bites at my lobe and murmurs, "Fucking you is going to be the highlight of my trip."

I hear the blood swishing through my ears and I'm so

wired my chest hurts.

He places a finger above each of my breasts then heats a trail to each nipple, circling until they are plump and hard. "And I'm definitely going to enjoy torturing these."

Kitty's purrs become deep and steady as the reality of what's about to happen overshadows my apprehension.

"Give me a sec." Branch steps away from me and flips on a light in the adjacent room, and I hear him taking a leak.

I sit on the edge of the bed and wonder if Hayley was right. Will I regret *not* doing this? And how will this all go down? Is he going to fuck me as if I'm one of his groupies? Will he only be concerned with his climax or will he make sure it's good for me? Either way, it will be hot as hell, so a release is definitely gonna occur on both sides. Hell, I nearly came when his lips grazed my ear. Chances are I'll detonate as soon as the tip touches kitty.

I hear the toilet flush and then the sound of running water. Moments later, Branch is standing in the doorway, lifting his shirt over his head and every part of me clenches tight. His body is sexy as sin and it takes everything in me not to gawk.

"Ready, sugar?"

"Stop calling me that."

"I thought *sugar* was a term of endearment. Should I try one of the less than sweet terms?" he asks, his voice a velvet whisper. "Do you like it dirty, Ragan? Is that what makes your cunt wet?"

Oh sweet fuck. I don't know if it's what I want but it definitely makes kitty go berserk! Screw the not gawking. I surrender to the urge and allow my gaze to flow over his body in successive waves. From his toned chest to his defined obliques, to the happy trail revealed by the loose belt and un-buttoned jeans.

Already aware of what his body is doing to me, he takes it a step further and reaches above his head and grips the door-frame, his muscles rippling and straining against thick veins, and I swear my ovaries explode.

I draw my eyes away from the perfect contours of muscle and meet his gaze. "Maybe I do like it dirty. And maybe my *cunt* is already wet."

His lips break into that arrogant smirk. "I expect it is and it's about to get a lot wetter," he replies and walks over to the side of the bed, reaches for my hand and pulls me to him. "You know you don't have to do this because of a dare."

"What makes you think that's the only reason I'm doing it? Maybe I want to give you a sample of what good pussy feels like."

A soft chuckle rumbles in his chest. "So this is Ragan high on liquid courage? I think I like it but darlin', don't make claims that little thing of yours can't back up. Every woman thinks her pussy is good."

"Maybe," I reply, the nerves replaced by the need to ex-perience the fantasy of being with this man. "Difference is, I speak the truth." I pull his head down to mine, halting any further conversation. And when our lips touch, it's all I want. He's all I want. Rough, dirty, sweet…however he chooses to give it, I want it. It's all I've wanted since he walked into the diner weeks ago. A few chance encounters and a lot of al-cohol may have brought me here, but now that I *am* here, I want him to fuck me with every ounce of aggression he dis-plays on the field. I want it all. I want *him*.

As if we are of one mind, he does precisely what I was

thinking. Without breaking our kiss, he moves me toward the bed. My fingers curve around his neck, drawing him closer and pressing his lips harder against mine. For a few seconds, he's right there with me but then he peels my hand away and peers down at me, his breathing in a pattern similar to mine.

"Sugar, I'm going to fuck you like there's no tomorrow. And then we're done. We leave here with no regrets. Agreed?"

I nod.

And then Branch McGuire lays me on the bed and covers my body with his.

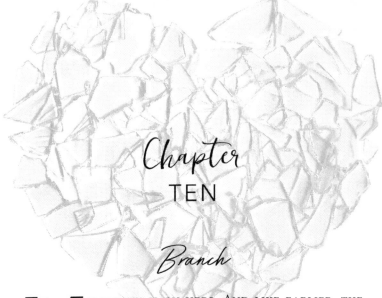

Chapter
TEN

Branch

MY MOUTH IS ON HERS. AND LIKE EARLIER, THE soft warmth of her lips triggers an emotion I don't recognize. My head is out of its element but my body responds as if on autopilot. I slip my hand under her shirt and palm her breast, kneading with firm squeezes as my erection grows harder with each stroke of my tongue against hers.

My free hand moves beneath her head to draw her mouth closer and to slide my tongue deeper. There's no hesitancy on her part—I didn't expect there would be. She wants this as badly, if not more so, than I do. And I feel it when it happens, when she totally surrenders her body to me, when she becomes hungry for whatever piece of me I'm willing to give. Just like all the others.

But it's my response that's unfamiliar. I struggle with a part of my brain. The part that always has one goal in mind when I'm with a woman—to use her body however I wish to satisfy my needs. To ravage her pussy and make it crave my dick long after it's gone.

But that part of my psyche is gradually falling to the background.

I don't understand why.

And why with Ragan?

I ignore the sirens in my head and permit my body to do what my mind can't comprehend. My hand trails along her curves, and with my thigh in between hers, I nudge them apart. When I reach the hotness between her legs, I massage and tease as the soft resonance of her moans fill my mouth. I never kiss the women I fuck, a fact that I've ignored tonight…until now. Until I break the kiss and move my lips along her cheek to the hollow of her neck, and breathe in the scent of her skin.

At her waist, I'm unbuttoning her jeans and lowering her zipper. And when I lift my body just enough, she shimmies out of the denim and her panties, then I'm back on top of her. Again falling out of character, my lips claim hers as I reposition my hand between her thighs.

Christ, she's wet. So fucking wet.

I trace a finger up and down her slit, heightening her arousal until those cock-throbbing moans of hers swallow us both. I then part her with my fingertip, moving between her seam—slow and purposeful until she's squirming beneath me. And not until she's desperate for more, do I press two fingers into the hot wet of her channel.

"Are you sure this is what you want?" I ask, her pussy greedy and clenching around my fingers as I work them back and forth. *I want her to want it.* But not just because of a dare and not because I'm Branch McGuire.

"Yes. Yes. Please," she replies, her words coming in breathy pants.

My fingers thrust inside the snug warmth of her tunnel, her legs open wider and her pelvis rocks into my hand. A motion that mirrors her words and pushes away every sexual guideline I've stuck to since high school. And unable to force them back to the surface, I drop deeper into foreign territory.

"Holy shit," she breathes. "What are you doing? Oh God. That feels amazing."

*If you think this is amazing…*with a slight twist of my hand, I curl the tips of my fingers as they move in and out, prompting her to connect harder and faster with my invasion. When I hit *that* spot, a soft cry escapes her lips. I continue working my fingers, moving deeper to stroke and caress the walls of her sex until vicious pulses signal her impending climax. Her hips buck in a desperate rhythm, reaching for it—but I won't let her come. Not like this. The first time she comes, it has to be with my dick inside her as the walls of her pussy tighten and relax to milk my release.

The thought of that impending connection extinguishes the remainder of my patience. I have to know what she feels like. I retract my fingers and rear back. Intent on filling her snug little tunnel with my cock, I spread her legs wider and the carnal aroma of her lust penetrates a part of me that's been long hidden. As if on instinct, I move down between her legs and breathe her in.

Fuck, she smells good. There's nothing like the sweet musky aroma of a wet pussy.

My mouth waters and then on a deeper inhale, I sweep my tongue between her lips, and damn if she doesn't taste like heaven. That one lick starts a frenzy of need…and a voracious hunger for her saccharine juices takes over.

My fingers move to spread her open and I dip deeper into the ocean between her legs, my tongue lapping to sate an unquenchable thirst.

Shit. I shouldn't be doing this. I summon the reserves of will power that demand I stop but the saline, honeyed fusion of her essence is an undeniable pleasure—one that elicits other long forgotten urges. Urges that won't allow me to stop.

My tongue snakes further into that sweet little hole that will soon be filled with something much larger. And unable to resist the tangy sweetness, I devour her—licking, sucking, fingering and tonguing as she clamps her thighs around my head.

She lets out a soft whimper and pushes into my mouth. Then my name is on her lips as she thrusts hard and fast against my tongue, the intensity of her lunges telling me she's almost there. And as much as I'd love the flow of her sweet nectar flooding my mouth, I'd much prefer my dick nestled inside the warmth of her pussy.

"Branch, oh...my...g—" Her words are lost when I position my tongue flat on her slit.

A slow lick up and then down, a soft flick back and forth and then she's writhing on my face, her climax again at its summit. She threads her fingers through my hair, her hands gripping the back of my head, her words a mix of soft whimpers and broken moans.

With noticeable reluctance, I abandon her pussy long enough for the seconds it takes to slip on the condom and then I watch her. She shudders as her orgasm makes a second attempt to stake its claim. I slide the pads of two fingers down her slit, preparing her for my entrance—another sign that I'm off my game. Yeah, the chick is usually primed and ready by the time I'm inside her, but I never give any thought to being sure that she is.

Ragan's legs fall apart, inviting me to do what we'd been dared. But this is no longer a game for me. *This is something I want.* I position myself between her thighs and slide the tip of my cock inside her. I pull out and in the next second, I push back in...but this time I go deeper.

Holy fucking shit. It's so hot. And so. fucking. good.

I look down at her, her lips are spread and her eyes are on my face.

I withdraw a third time, wanting to prolong this, but I already know there's no fucking way that will happen. I drive my length to the end of her and she lets out a gasp.

I need to take it slower.

Moving at this pace is fucking killing me but I force myself to ease her into it, rotating my hips, massaging the walls of her sex, allowing her to adjust to my girth with each move, and finally when she's stretched around me, I push all the way in, my pelvis flush with hers.

Her exhale is unsteady as she breathes through my plunges, her hands gripping my arms and pulling me to her chest.

"Damn," I whisper, my mouth skirts along her jaw as I start to move as deep as her pussy will allow. I didn't expect her cunt to clench so tightly around my cock, not like this. It's enough to make me lose my load right now. I pull out to the tip and groan as I press back in. Two more thrusts and I'm convinced this is where I belong—buried inside her.

"Ragan." I can't say more, the unfamiliar friction of our bodies writhing like savages has taken my words. I grind my hips against hers, rooting my cock even further inside a pussy I don't want to withdraw from.

How the fuck can she feel this good?

Hell, I don't want to stop. I can go all night with Ragan and still want more—which is fucking mind-blowing because I've never felt that way about any other woman. Her pussy is *that* good. And there's a sweetness about her, a vulnerability that fuels the adrenaline rushing through my body.

With my forehead pressed against hers, I pick up the pace, each plunge hitting the depth of her.

"Oh, shit. Right there," she pants. "Oh fuck…don't stop. Please."

But I do stop. "I want you completely naked. Take everything off," I whisper.

"Why?" Her voice is a breathy gasp.

"Because I said so." *Why the fuck is she questioning me now of all times?*

She hesitates, and I get that she's apprehensive about her body. I sensed that when I touched her on the field. But I want to see and touch every part of her. "Do it, Ragan."

I rear back when she reaches for the tail of her shirt and lifts it over her head, her breathing still labored as she removes her bra and slings it on the bed beside us. She reclines with her arms covering the parts she doesn't wish for me to see, but that's the opposite of what I want. I position her hands above her head and meet her eyes. I see the uncertainty. I see the insecurity. And when my gaze moves over her body, I see the beauty I know she's unaware of.

Her breasts, although heavy with yearning, are perky and tight—the precise size to fit within the grasp of my palm. And sitting at the crown of each, are nipples plump with lust.

Her stomach—the area she's most self-conscious about—isn't toned, but it blends perfectly with the thickness of her thighs and the curve of her hips. My eyes trace upwards, focused on the outline that shapes her body into a perfect hourglass and my erection stiffens inside her.

I trail my hands along her legs, over her thighs, past her stomach and then grasp her tits. "I'm going to show you what your body is made for." I dip down and trace my tongue over each nipple as my dick moves in and out of her snug little channel.

"Ahh," she breathes.

"Feel good?"

"Mmm-hmm." Her breath hitches as the tips of her breasts harden.

"Oh, sugar. It gets better." I draw a nipple into my mouth, my teeth grazing the tight pebble as I start to suck. My lips are splayed over the swollen bead as I pull—the suction tight so that it elicits both pain and pleasure. When I deliver the same treatment to her other breast, her pants become louder, filling the room as she forgoes her insecurities and arches into my mouth.

I release her breast with a pop and go for the other while I squeeze, twist and pull the tip of the one I abandoned.

"Kiss me," she whispers. "Please kiss me."

I nip her bottom lip, our breaths mingled as I wrestle with indecision. Her sexy little noises hover between us, hardening my cock into stone, then my mouth is smothering hers, our lips moving, teeth clashing and tongues dueling as the kiss deepens. Her nails are at my back, scoring my skin and my hands trail down her body, my fingers digging into her thighs as I race toward my release, feeling hers chasing closely behind.

She feels fucking incredible. I want to draw this out. Dammit, I *need* to, but I can't stop.

I go harder.

And deeper.

Knowing it will push me to the point I'm trying to steer away from.

"Ahh, yes. Branch. Right there," she whimpers, her hands on my skin, her pussy clenching…tighter.

She bucks and writhes beneath me. "Don't stop. Please, don't stop."

"I don't plan on it," I murmur, as my hips grind viciously against hers.

Her breathy moans pull at my release and I whisper against her ear. "You feel so good wrapped around me."

Her body becomes rigid and I whisper more, "My dick feels so good nestled inside you. I intend to fuck you until you're too sore to walk."

And she whispers back, her words searing my skin, "You're stretching me and it hurts…but it feels so good."

My dick throbs for a release as I move deeper inside her. Her hands trail down my back, cupping my ass and squeezing.

"Oh fuck, your cock is so…ahh…good."

Her words quicken my pace. I ram into her with a rapid aggression that moves the headboard to a rhythm of its own, knocking against the wall as she bites into my shoulder.

When the need to come pulls on me again, I take her slower. I swivel my hips and rotate my cock inside her, and then fuck if she doesn't squeeze me, the walls of her sex grip me so tight I nearly come undone.

"Sugar, you're gonna make me come if you keep doing that."

"Isn't that the point?" she breathes.

"Eventually," I whisper with a grunt and push back into her, slow and deep. "But not now."

"I told you my pussy was good," she says and her hips rock up, rotating her cunt on the ridge of my cock when I pull out.

"Shit," I groan, hovering over the brink of my climax. I move the crown of my dick up and down her seam before pushing into her again and exhale a breath. When my cock is once again perfectly cocooned in the tight warmth of her cunt, I know there's no way I'll stop fucking her. No fucking way.

"Shit, Ragan. You feel so goddamn good." My hips buck into hers, and establish a steady rhythm. And it's too good. I can't hold it. I tell myself to pull out or at least slow down, but that shit ain't happening. A low groan forms in my chest as my restraint evaporates.

"I want you to come with me. Think you can do that?"

"I'm already there. Fuck, I'm already there," she pants, her words muffled by the hitch in her throat.

I want to look down at her, but my own release seizes me, then I'm throwing my head back, pouring into her with a series of fierce grunts, then held captive to an orgasm that has no end—it's the longest and hardest I've come in my entire fucking life.

After a short intermission, I've flipped her over, pulled her to her knees and I'm pounding her doggy style, my thighs slapping against her delightfully round ass as she begs me not to stop. She needn't worry about that because I don't intend to. Her cries become louder, her words more erotic, and my dick harder. I know everyone in the place hears her with one hundred percent clarity but that does nothing to deter me. I plan to fuck her until the sun rises.

Some hours later, I reach around and rub her clit as my dick slams into her, our final orgasms erupting in tandem. Mine with a low growl and hers with an elongated cry.

Undeniably spent, I collapse on top of her, my weight on her body as we fight to catch our breath. I don't let her go. And I don't turn away from the kiss she asks for.

I don't do this type of shit.

Something isn't right, and I still can't figure out what the hell it is.

I wasn't rough with her.

At least not as rough as I could have been.

I was attentive, almost tender…something I didn't think I was capable of being to any woman. Except Madison…and that was a time in my past I left in the past. I could possibly deal with all of the odd shit I'd done with Ragan, but to go down on her? What the hell was that? Before last night, I was pretty fucking positive that it'd be a cold day in hell before my tongue felt the inside of *any* pussy. Obviously I was wrong as shit about that. And what makes it worse, she hadn't asked for it. I'd wanted it. Fuck, I had to practically negotiate with myself to stop.

And now, mere minutes after it's all over I'm lying beside her, missing the feel of her pussy clenched around me. And to top it all off, *I'm fucking snuggling.* For a guy who never does any of this shit with any chick, I'm batting a thousand with Ragan.

What the fuck?

With the light of morning it's as though we don't know what to say. And the side of me that usually wants to push a woman out the door doesn't surface. I want Ragan to hang around. I look over at her and deny the impulse to pull her close, to stroke her hair, to kiss her.

I see the awkward smile on her face and realize she's uncomfortable. And fuck if I don't feel the same. A reminder that we need to stick to our agreement. One night. No regrets. Move on.

"You good?" I ask.

"Yeah." She grimaces. "Extremely sore but otherwise I'm okay."

She looks as if she wants to say more but doesn't.

"Something wrong?" I ask as I move to pull on my jeans.

"I'm a little surprised I guess."

"About what?"

"You." She sits up in bed, resting on her elbows.

"What about me?"

"I knew it would be amazingly hot. And it was. Like this incredible sheet-grasping, hair-pulling experience. But it was more than that actually. You were both what I expected and what I didn't expect at the same time."

"And how did you expect me to be?"

"I don't know. You're very..." she starts and then fades off again as if she's searching for the right words. "I guess I thought it would be like some rough porno night...but it wasn't."

My brow arches. "Is that what you wanted?"

"To be honest, I think that's what I was looking for. Until you touched me, then it all changed."

Yeah, it all changed for me too, but it shouldn't have.

"Maybe now, I understand why women like Skye aren't too proud to beg."

"Whoa." I hold up my palms in defense. "Wait a minute, Ragan. Last night…what happened between us…that's not… that wasn't the norm."

"So you have a list of services?" she asks playfully, a side of her I don't typically see. "Which one did I get?"

"It's not like that. There's no list. I'm gonna be dead honest here. I don't know what the fuck happened last night. The version of me you expected is the version *all* women get."

"Oh," she says. "I don't get it. May I ask—"

"I don't do questions."

"What about answers? Do you *do* those?" she asks, an edge to her voice.

I slip my shirt over my head. "Nope."

"Don't you think that's a little—"

"We agreed to fuck and that's it. We're done here, Ragan."

A blush shades her cheeks, then her expression shifts to the one I've seen many days at the diner in response to my asshole moves. "I guess we are," she says as I grab my shoes and open the door.

"See you around," I say, cutting ties with the last several hours and with the woman I don't plan to see ever again.

Chapter
ELEVEN

Ragan

I SOMEHOW MANAGE TO ARRIVE AT THE DINER ONLY A few minutes after my shift starts. Well, in body at least. Waiting tables isn't my calling, that's for sure. But if breaking fewer glasses and plates is any measure of improvement, I've gotten better. I'm sure Jim Bob sees it that way, so yeah, I've gotten better. But this morning, it's as if I've reverted to day one. All thumbs. A slip of a glass here, drop of a plate there, and it's back to Jim Bob's threats of cutting my check. *Fuck*.

Last night's drinking was draining within itself, but everything that happened afterward is pulling at every available brain cell that isn't needed to move through the motions of taking orders, wiping tables and serving customers. And each time the door opens, I find myself risking whiplash to see if it's Branch. But it's never Branch, and when the Coca-Cola clock shows a little past two, I accept that he isn't coming.

As badly as I need to forget about him *and* last night, I can't if I wanted to—each step meets me with a tender ache. He said he'd fuck me until I was too sore to walk and dammit if he didn't do just that. And if I didn't have to be at Jim Bob's right now, I'd let kitty soak the day away in a nice hot bath.

I hear Branch's final words to me. They are on repeat.

"We agreed to fuck and that's it. We're done here, Ragan."

"See you around."

Yeah, I could get beyond that because it's no less than what I agreed to…twice. He even gave me an out before anything happened but I didn't take it. Okay, so maybe it's *all* difficult to swallow but the one thing he said that leaves me conflicted is, "*What happened between us…that wasn't the norm.*"

Why was it different with me? Was it because I *wasn't* like the others, so he couldn't do to me what he did to them? That's the only thing that makes sense. I don't know whether to feel embarrassed or shortchanged.

Shortchanged? Nah. Wrong word. He was *amazing*. I mean *really* amazing. And he ate my pussy like it was his profession. Maybe he should get two hundred fifty million for *that*.

But he said, I didn't get what I expected. What the hell did that mean? Maybe it was best he didn't come to the diner today…or any day. Last night needs to be exactly what we agreed. A one-time thing with no regrets. Yeah, I could live with that.

Or could I?

As the day draws on, I start to question that more and more because Branch is crowding my thoughts. He's pushing everything out of my brain except him. And the same question is rolling around in my head…over and over. Why had Branch been different with me? And if the porno version is his *norm*, did I receive the *nice* version? My nipples are basically raw and kitty is damn near the same so I don't know how *nice* it was, but it was hella good. The man has skills, I'll give him that. But what prompted the change in the bedroom? I mean, he's been a dick pretty much every day since he's come back to town. So why shift gears last night? Not like he's the nicest person in the world, so I certainly didn't expect him to be nice in bed. Did he think I couldn't handle the full rawness that was Branch McGuire? Or maybe he'd shown the side of himself he hadn't intended for me to see. Fuck, I don't know.

It was definitely a side I would have sworn didn't exist. And that makes me even more curious about a man I will never have. So maybe it will end up being a regret after all. Another alcohol-laced evening. One he'll forget and one I'll always remember.

The diner is near capacity and I can't do much more than kick into robot mode. No more thoughts of Branch, only greasy food and refills on sweet tea. When Carrie comes in, I say hi and head to the back to put my feet up. On the way to the breakroom, I stop at my locker for my cell to call Aunt Sophie and check in on CeeCee. After about five minutes of searching every pocket *and* the small hole in my purse, I realize I don't have my phone.

"Oh shit." The last place I remember having it was at the cabin. I use the phone in the diner to call Hayley asking if she by chance grabbed my cell. She replies in the negative and then she's talking ninety to nothing, asking a steady stream of questions about last night. I tell her I'll call her later when

I'm home, then I go to Jim Bob's office and explain I need to use his computer. Surprisingly enough, he allows it, albeit for ten minutes, but that should be all I need. After a series of Facebook friend requests, I finally get in touch with Darcy and she says I'm welcome to check the cabin and tells me where I can find the spare key.

At the end of my shift, I take the half-hour drive up to Morganton and after a few wrong turns, I finally come upon the cabin. Darcy mentioned I may not need the key because a cleaning crew was coming out today. Guess they made it because a dark gray SUV was parked out front.

I hop out of the car and walk along the pebble walkway stepping stones as I scan the space, noting how it all looks so differently in the light of day. The cabin is a two-story structure surrounded by several tall pine trees that add to the backwoodsiness appeal of the place. The upper level boasts a spacious deck with massive log-framed windows. Aside from the pine needles, a few leaves and scattered pinecones, the lawn is perfectly landscaped. The final touch is the ever-green shrubbery running along the front length of the lower deck. The scenery is practically a beautiful picturesque post-card come to life—countryside elegance at its best.

I walk up the steps and knock at the large wooden door, but no answer. For a moment, I think I'm at the wrong place until I spot Darcy's last name engraved on the oval placard a few feet to the left of the door. And funny how I don't re-member the stairs even though this morning I traipsed down them to head back to town. I imagine Branch, Matt, Darcy and the rest of their group have a lot of awesome memories from their teenage days at this place. I'm a little saddened knowing that. I've always been on the outside looking in. But last night I was actually on the inside, and that didn't turn out so well either. Maybe because I wasn't really one of the insiders.

After a second knock, I go for the key, looking in the place Darcy mentioned, but it's not there. I try the opposite side and locate the key lodged inside the small grayish stone at the base of a planter.

I unlock the door, replace the key, then step inside the cabin. As I glance around the rustically furnished room, nothing looks familiar. Last night I was coasting on beer and the high of being in Branch's proximity, so I paid very little attention to most everything else. I shake off that high school girl and remember the last place I had my phone was in the plush sofa near the fireplace. As I'm digging in the cushions, I hear a noise from behind the closed door on the far side of the room. I ignore it and continue my search. Just as I start to get frustrated, I feel my phone and pull it from the sofa. After checking the status of the battery life on my cell, I slip it into my pocket.

Relieved that I found what I came for, I start to head out but the strange sound coming from across the room once again grasps my attention. Thinking it's the cleaning crew, I redirect my steps, curious as to why they don't hear me and why they didn't respond when I knocked on the door.

Chapter
TWELVE

Ragan

I CRACK THE DOOR OPEN, THEN EXPEL A SILENT GASP.

I'm literally too stunned to move.

The scene unfolding before my eyes is truly sickening.

She's in front of him on her knees. As his cock stands at attention.

And holy shit, he's huge. I'd felt him inside me and I'd known he was well endowed but I hadn't seen *all* of him until now. No wonder I'm sore as shit—his cock is a fucking anaconda. And now I'm standing here, inexplicably adhered to this spot as some blonde prepares to blow what had been buried in me just a few hours ago.

Her mouth meets the head of his penis with a kiss and then she edges closer, curving her fingers around his length, grasping the base and then twirling. Her efforts apparently coax evidence of his arousal to the surface, because her tongue goes in for a dip. Then his hands come up and grab her hair, guiding her. Following his lead, she moves forward and feeds his erection past her lips, slowly moving down, struggling to swallow him whole.

On the second long suck he lets out a hiss. Then the blonde picks up the pace, her head bobbing up and down with a rapidity that suggests she's starved for his seed.

And he meets her with each plunge, his dick bucking in and out of her mouth at a steady rhythm.

No. No. No. I tell myself I shouldn't watch this and a sinking feeling in my belly urges me to step back, close the door, turn around and get the hell out of this cabin. But I don't move. My feet aren't listening. And I can't look away, so I watch. I've become a voyeur…the unwilling type.

His hands are still gripping her hair. Still guiding her.

The woman doesn't stop. Her head bobs faster, her mouth greedy and desperate for his climax. His hips rock up to meet her, his thrusts coming faster and harder. There's no compassion in his expression, no concern for her, just his own selfish need. I see it plain as day as the woman gives it her all, downing gag after gag with deep sucks as she's mercilessly face fucked by Branch McGuire.

My heart rate quickens and my stomach lurches as I wait in the shadows for his orgasm. And with a low grunt, when he's taken from her all that he can, he lets go, spilling into her mouth. He looks down at the blonde, his expression cloaked with pleasure as my throat clenches and a warm feeling rises through my chest, then I taste the bile in the back of my mouth.

At the peak of his release, he emits a low guttural sound that I feel across the room. The blonde motions to pull back but his hands clutch the sides of her head as he forces his release down her throat.

And she swallows the prize…all of it.

At the last pull, his hands relax and she looks up at him. "Are you going to fuck me now?" she asks. Or I suppose that's what she asked. I couldn't really make out what she said, so my imagination filled in that part.

Branch urges her back, then he stands, his cock still hard.

I gasp, and that's when they notice me.

It's *her*. I should have known…Skye Jamison.

She flashes me a taunting smile. Then my eyes fly to his and for milliseconds they connect—my browns to his blues. And then as if recovering from the shock themselves, my feet finally take the order my brain has been screaming. I step back, do an about-face, and bolt from the cabin.

Chapter
THIRTEEN

Branch

W*HAT THE FUCK IS SHE DOING HERE?* "Ragan! Wait!"

She doesn't. *Of course, she doesn't.*

Instead, the door slams behind her.

Skye ignores the interruption, taking me in her mouth, and not breaking the suction on my cock until I nudge her head away. "Goddamnit, stop." I shove myself back into my boxers and hurry out behind Ragan.

When I reach the deck, she's already halfway down the drive. "Ragan!"

I may as well have been yelling at the wind because she doesn't slow her stride nor does she look back. Forgoing shoes or clothes, I hurry down the steps after her. She comes to a stumbling halt near the front of her car, buckles over and hurls.

Oh, shit. This situation is royally fucked.

"Ragan! Can we talk?"

She runs the back of her hand over her mouth and looks up at me. When I'm a few feet away, she jumps in the car and backs out of the drive.

"Ragan," I yell again, but it's useless. "Fuck!"

I rush back inside for the keys to Matt's SUV, and Skye meets me at the door. *Naked*. "We're leaving."

"But—"

"Get dressed."

She follows me across the room. "Are you kidding me?"

"Either get dressed and let's go or find another ride back to town." I pull on my clothes, grab my phone, and head out the door. Within seconds I'm in the SUV punching the horn for Skye and seriously considering leaving her the fuck here.

I grab my phone to call Ragan, but realize her number is not in my list of contacts. "Shit."

In a huff, Skye jumps in the SUV, her shirt unbuttoned and her shoes in hand. "Are we seriously done?"

I shake my head at her and spin the vehicle around, pissed that Skye is beside me, pissed that I give a fuck what Ragan thinks and pissed that I'm in Blue Ridge. I toss the phone on the seat and slam my fist against the steering wheel.

"You *actually* have a thing for her, don't you?" Skye asks, her tone incredulous.

My jaws clench. And my eyes remain focused on the road.

Ignoring speed limits and rolling through stop signs, I reduce the half-hour drive from Morganton to ten minutes.

"Where's your house?"

Skye rattles off her address and I'm at her place in no time, screeching to a stop at the foot of her driveway with the door barely closing behind her before I set off in the direction of Ragan's.

I pull up and hop out of the SUV just as she's getting out of the car.

"Ragan, wait."

She spins around and glares at me, her eyes tear-stained. And my gut pulls tight. I did this to her. I knew it was a mistake to fuck her. *I fucking knew it.*

"Done already?" she snaps. "You weren't up for giving her the hours you gave to me? Guess I lucked out, huh?"

"Nothing happened." *Shit, why am I explaining to her?*

"Maybe in your douchebag world, fucking someone in the mouth is 'nothing', but here in Real World, Georgia, it's a hell of a lot more than that."

"Nothing happened besides that, I mean."

"Whether it did or didn't, it's really none of my business. Besides, isn't that what you do—go from one woman to the next without pause? But I would have thought you'd at least give it a day between different pussies."

Ouch. She's right. On both counts. But it's not like I went looking for it—I hopped in the shower and when I came out of the bathroom, I discovered she was the last one at the cabin. And Skye being Skye, she was down for whatever I wanted. I never go back for seconds, but I made an exception. The motive—fucking one woman to forget about the one I never should have touched. *Total dick move, McGuire.*

"I know you think I'm a piece of shit. And maybe I am but—"

"Maybe?" She scoffs and turns away from me.

"Fuck, Ragan. Can you give me five minutes?"

Surprisingly enough, she stops. Her shoulders rise and fall on an exhale before turning around to face me.

"What you walked in on...that has nothing to do with you."

"Obviously," she sneers. "It wasn't my mouth wrapped around your dick, so how could it possibly have anything to do with me?"

"That's not what I meant and you damn well know it," I reply, my temper rising again.

"Let me save you the hassle of spitting out some lame explanation. I don't care. You don't owe me shit. Nor do I owe you. We did the deed. We said one night and no regrets. Well, that night is over and I have zero regret. You've got four minutes left."

She's giving me the time I asked for but as I look at her, I realize I don't know what I was planning to say. What *can* I say? I told myself, I'd never see her again, so why the fuck am I asking to explain something that actually *is* none of her business? But what if this is my fault? Have I been leading her on? Did we both make an agreement we shouldn't have? Shit if I know.

I toss up my hands in frustration. "Just forget it. I don't know why I'm even here."

"Neither do I. As a matter of fact, why not make this easier on both of us? Can you skip the diner?"

My brows furrow. "Come again."

"Let's keep our distance. No more lunches at the diner, dinners at Jimmy's, boat rides or anything."

Best idea I've heard all fucking day. "Suits me just fine. I don't need the trouble."

"Likewise."

Chapter
FOURTEEN

Ragan

IF THE SHEER WILL TO PUSH SOMEONE FROM YOUR thoughts was all it took to make it happen, my head would be Branch-free, but wishing it doesn't make it so. Every moment of the last few days is a movie reel with a critic echoing each highlight of my twisted weekend.

Not that I count it as solace but at least now I know what Branch meant when he said I didn't get the *norm*. Having witnessed his cruelty to Skye, I guess I really *should* consider myself lucky. He wasn't at all like that with me. It was obvious that pleasing me was important to him—that he wanted me to get off as often as he did. So why…why did he get with *her* just hours after? And why chase me down to explain?

I let out a sigh and glance up from the circles I was tracing on the counter and meet the cold hard eyes of Ethan Tyler.

"I need to see my daughter."

Just fucking great. I think I actually hate this man. And if I don't, I know I should. "Kind of like I *need* the child support you promised."

He leans over the counter and says in a low voice, "So you're gonna hold my kid hostage until you get a check out of me?"

"Am I going to have to take you to court to make you do what you *should* be doing anyway?"

"As if you could afford a lawyer," he taunts. "I'm pretty positive all the money you had when you left me is gone, otherwise you wouldn't be living with your piece-of-shit dad and working in this dump."

"Screw you, Ethan. Do you think you're some huge success story? Just because you have a job at a fucking fish company and work hour after hour of overtime for extra money? And for what? Just to prove to yourself that you've made it?"

"You sure didn't mind when I was spending that *extra* money on you. And I'll take smelling like fish and bringing home the money I make any day over this shit," he says, gesturing around the diner.

"You mean the money you refuse to spend on your child? You're a real asshole."

"When CeeCee is with me, she has whatever she wants. Money is not a problem."

"But that's not what you promised and you know it." Realizing this conversation is useless, I shake my head. "You know what? Forget it…I'm not going back and forth with you about this. Just know your day is coming. I may be down on my luck—happens to the best of us—but make no mistake, I'll bounce back and I'll be coming for you, you son of a bitch."

He scoffs. "Yeah, good luck with that."

The door chime sounds and my eyes track across the diner and fall on Branch McGuire. For long seconds, my eyes rest in his, anger and embarrassment filling every part of me as I recall my last encounter with him.

Ethan follows my gaze, then spins around on the bar stool and lets out a mocking chuckle. "If you think you stand a chance of someone like him doing anything more than looking at you like you're the dirt under his shoe, you've lost your mind. Baby, I'm the best you're *ever* gonna get."

As Carrie greets Branch and directs him to a table, I reply to Ethan. "That's not saying very much. Besides, who says I don't already have better?"

Confusion washes over his features before his face falls into a scowl. "What the fuck did you say?"

"You heard me."

His brows shoot up. "Are you actually fucking someone?"

"What's between my legs belongs to me. If I want to let someone have it, that's my choice."

Ethan's palm lands across my cheek, then he grips my upper arm, pulling me around the counter and closer to him. "Bitch, if I ever see you with another man, you're dead. Do you hear me?"

His voice is hard and menacing, his eyes heated. His threat pushes me back to the brutalizing days with Cassidy—the paralyzing fear, stuttering heartbeats and the feeling of being trapped in something I can't get out of. But this is not Cassidy and I'm not trapped. I refuse to kowtow to Ethan, not like I did in the past.

My hand balls into a tight fist and connects with Ethan's jaw, and he nearly falls from the stool.

Shock and anger register in his expression. "What the hell's gotten into you?" His fingers curl tighter around my arm.

"Get your damn hands off of me," I whisper through clenched teeth.

"You used to love my hands on you," he sneers, pulling me to his chest. "And you know what? I think you still do." He tugs me behind him, damn near dragging me out of the diner.

"Dammit, Ethan, let me go."

"You've proved your point. You walked away from me, from the life I was trying to give to you. But I know you still love me and this bullshit stops today. You're coming home with me."

I yank my arm, attempting to escape his grasp, but his grip shows no mercy, hurting me and forcing my steps behind him. When we reach Ethan's Jeep, he opens the door and with his hand at my waist he shoves me toward the passenger seat. My fingers curve around the door frame in resistance to his brute strength.

"Get in the damn car," he yells.

"You can't force me to want you. Let me go, Ethan!"

He jerks my wrist and my hand abandons the frame of the car and goes for his face, my nails swiping the flesh of his cheek.

"You fucking cunt!" he lets out, with a jab to my abdomen. The air leaves my lungs in a rush and when I keel over, he shoves me into the car. "This is gonna happen, so stop fighting me," he snarls.

I'm on my back with the weight of his body pressing onto mine and forcing my hip against the console. My legs roust with his until I gain the leeway to land a knee to his balls. He lets out a yelp, then rears back. I feel the next blow even before it happens. I brace myself, my lids squeezed tight and my forearms crossed over my face.

But the strike doesn't come.

I open my eyes and find him pinned against his car. And Branch is holding his forearm against Ethan's throat.

"Get the fuck off me, man," Ethan demands.

"I should choke the living shit out of you," Branch says. "I guess exerting your power over a defenseless woman makes you feel like a big man."

"If you knew what the fuck you were talking about, you'd know Ragan is not defenseless. She's a fucking whore, man."

Branch responds with an uppercut to Ethan's solar plexus, landing his head against the side of the car. "Is that right? Is that why you're forcing her to do something she doesn't want to do? I thought whores were *eager* for their johns."

Branch closes the space between the two of them, his forearm resting underneath Ethan's chin, and pinning him tighter against the car.

"This ain't your business," Ethan chokes out. "You don't know shit about me."

"Yeah, but I'm about to."

Ethan struggles to no avail to escape Branch's grip. "You don't fucking scare me."

"You don't need to be scared, do you?"

"I said, get the fuck off of me," Ethan barks, scrambling to shake Branch's hold.

I clamber out of the car and although I should move as far away from Ethan as fast as I can, I don't. His loss of control has me frozen in place. I've never seen him like this. And I'm afraid of what's coming next. It's like something inside of him has snapped. I take a few paces back.

"Hey, you bitch, come back here," Ethan barks after me.

Ignoring his order, I take a few more steps.

"Fine. You run, but I promise I'll see you later. You can count on that."

Branch yanks Ethan's collar, bringing them face to face. "If you so much as walk on the same side of the street as she does, you piece of shit, I'll find you and make it very hard for you to breathe."

"Man, fuck you."

Branch throws a right cross, landing Ethan on the ground beside his Jeep. Before I can make heads or tails of what's happening, Branch is on top of him and they roll back and forth, one trying to gain footing over the other. Branch fists Ethan's shirt, holding him in place and then his knuckles pummel Ethan's jaw.

Out of nowhere comes the crew of guys Branch usually comes into the diner with, and they're ripping the two men apart. Ethan scrambles to his feet, spitting blood. He looks at the others and then he looks at me.

"If you think this is over—"

"Oh, it's over," Branch warns. "Get the hell out of here."

Ethan spits again, then a malicious grin spreads over his lips. After one final glance at me, he gets in his car and spins out of the parking lot.

The guys toss out questions at Branch, but he doesn't respond. His eyes are still on me. And the pity in his expression pulls more tears than Ethan's blow to my abdomen. What the hell is Branch doing here anyway? Was he not listening to the part where he agreed to keep his distance from me? Turning away with my arm cradling my midsection, I shove past the onlookers and rush inside the diner.

Chapter
FIFTEEN

Ragan

JUST AS I STEP BEHIND THE COUNTER, JIM BOB APPEARS and pulls me into his office. After he confirms I'm okay, he announces he's calling the police. I literally pry the phone from his hand, then plead with him to let this go. It takes some convincing but he reluctantly agrees to let me handle Ethan my way. After an apology for not being around when Ethan showed up, Jim Bob swears my ex won't be allowed in the diner again.

As thankful as I am to hear those words and to see the outrage that twists my boss's expression, it does little to assure me that I'll be safe from that monster. His control and abuse were always subtle and *private*. His public display is a clear indication that he's lost his fucking mind.

Jim Bob's gaze trails over the mark on my cheek, my forearm enclosing my abdomen, then the tattered cloth of my uniform. With that same pitiable look in his eyes as Branch, he tells me to go home, get some rest, and come in tomorrow afternoon if I feel up to it. I don't bother contradicting him. Between the embarrassment of my appearance and the incident itself, I want to bury my head in the sand.

I step into the house, my fingers trembling as I turn the deadbolt on the door…still terrified Ethan will make good on his threat. I'm actually shocked I made it to Dad's unscathed. For nearly the entire fifteen-mile drive, my eyes were on the rearview mirror when they should have been on the road. And now that I'm home I need, more than anything else, to see my daughter, to focus on the joy of her innocence and to forget the mistakes and naïveté of a past that continues to wreak havoc in my life.

Dad is sitting in his recliner, his eyes glued to whatever is playing out on *ESPN*. "Hi, Dad."

"Hey, Ragan. How was work?" he asks, his gaze steadfast on the TV.

"It's a diner, so that tells you all you need to know," I reply. "Where's CeeCee?"

"What do you mean?" He finally looks up, his brows scrunched as he takes in my appearance.

"CeeCee usually runs to me for a hug as soon as I step in the house. Don't tell me you guys let her nap early again."

"Did you forget that you told Ethan he could have her for the night? He left with her a little while ago."

A nervous tickling traces my gut. "He did what?"

"He said he'd stopped by the diner and made sure everything was still a go."

I go for my cell, then hit Ethan's number. The phone rings and rings and rings, then goes to voicemail. I call again. And again. "Son of a bitch."

Aunt Sophie appears from the hall carrying a basket of laundry, her steps faltering as her gaze trails over me. "What's going on, Ragan?"

"Were you here when Ethan came to get Cecelia?" I ask.

"Yes, I packed a bag for her."

"Are you kidding me?"

"Ethan said you were running late for work today and didn't have time to pack it."

"You didn't," I accuse.

"Well, you *are* always running late, Ragan, so I didn't see anything odd with his explanation," she said. "What's wrong and what happened to your face?" Her eyes roll over me a second time. "And your uniform?"

"Ethan is what's wrong and Ethan is what happened to my face and my clothes. I can't believe you let him take my daughter."

Tears are spilling from my eyes and I'm damn near sobbing by the time I dial 911 and give the operator details of Ethan's disappearance with CeeCee. Uncle Stan walks into the room with a single can of beer in one hand and the entire case tucked under his arm. Aunt Sophie fills him in as I step into the kitchen to answer the operator's questions.

Minutes later, I'm outside. In between pacing the driveway and waiting for the police, I'm dialing Ethan's phone over and over but only getting voicemail. I start calling anyone on my contact list who could have any type of connection to Ethan, starting with his mom—the woman who once claimed me as a daughter.

"Have you seen Ethan?" I ask as soon as she answers.

"I sure have...and my granddaughter, too. No thanks to you."

The abrasive edge in her tone is another gash to a fresh wound. "Marjorie, I'm not sure what that means and right now I don't care. I've been calling Ethan for over an hour but he's not picking up. Can you put him on the phone?"

"I said, I *saw* him. Past tense. He's not here and neither is Cecelia."

My short-lived relief shifts back to all-out panic. "Where are they?"

"Why would I tell you? So you can go and snatch his daughter out of his arms? Not gonna happen, sweet cheeks."

"Look, I don't have time for this, Marjorie. I need to find my daughter. Ethan took her without my permission."

She scoffs. "He's Cecelia's father. How do you figure he needs *permission* to see his own child?"

"He can't just take her whenever he feels like it, especially if it's just to get back at me."

"Get back at you for what? For making a fool of him?"

"What are you talking about?"

"I guess I shouldn't be surprised considering how you were raised," she says, the judgment in her tone taking me by surprise. "He told me everything. Now I know why you were so gung ho about leaving him."

"You know why Ethan and I are not together anymore. You yourself told me you saw signs in him that reminded you of his dad, and that I should leave him, so don't even try this shit with me."

"Watch your mouth, young lady. And maybe I was wrong. Especially after hearing how you'd been cheating on my son."

"Cheating on Ethan? Is that what he told you? He cheated on *me*!" I yell into the phone. "Multiple times."

"We took you in and treated you like family. And this is how you repay us? By telling lies on my boy and keeping Cecelia away from us? And Lord knows what else you're up to these days. You'll probably end up a drugged-out prostitute like your mother. My son is better off without a whore like you and so is my granddaughter," she says, then the line goes quiet.

I dial her back, but the phone doesn't ring. It goes straight to voicemail. I start to redial just as the police pull to a stop at the foot of the driveway.

"Finally," I say and run to the patrol car.

As one of the officers pulls out a pad, I tell him about Ethan taking my daughter, and although I'd decided against it earlier, I also tell them about his assaulting me at the diner. Their reply is not at all what I expected. They say unless I have papers that state otherwise, Ethan is full within his rights. They also say I need to come downtown tomorrow to file a report about what occurred at the diner.

Dad, Uncle Stan, and Aunt Sophie are beside me asking their own questions but the answers are the same—there's nothing I can do but wait until Ethan brings CeeCee home. The officer who'd been quiet up to this point, pulls out a card and passes it to me, suggesting I contact the abuse counselor if I need to talk to someone. And that's it. I watch as they get in the car and pull away. Disheartened by the mechanical response from the police, I turn toward the house, shocked to see the sympathy in Aunt Sophie's eyes as she pulls me into a hug, then walks me back inside.

For hours we sit around the kitchen table, repeatedly

calling anyone Ethan may know, only to get one dead end after another. I leave message after message on his phone and when exhaustion finally pulls me under, I rest my head on the table. Less than a minute later, my lids fall like dead weight to a reluctant slumber.

The following morning I awake to muscle aches and stiffness. The scuffle with Ethan coupled with an uncomfortable night's sleep pretty much guarantee a hellish day but denying physical pain is nothing new to me, and even if it wasn't, it would still take a back seat to locating my daughter.

My gaze crawls over the still of the kitchen as the pang of emptiness settles in. My daughter's gone. I'm left with no mother, a piece of a father, and a temperamental aunt. As my eyes start to water, it hits me—there's no one who'll fight for me. And with CeeCee gone, I have no one to fight for.

The family I thought I'd found in Ethan's has crumbled to nothing—I can only imagine the horrible lies he told Marjorie about me. Why else would she turn on me with such vicious judgment?

I don't understand why this is happening. Why is it that every time I feel even the tiniest bit of hope, it's snatched away from me? Why?

Three days pass.

No word from Ethan.

I take a chance and go to Marjorie's, hoping some sort of maternal disposition will persuade her to place our differences aside for the betterment of my daughter, but when she looks out and sees me at the door, she closes the blinds. A tornado of emotions swirl in my gut at her betrayal and disregard of me, as not only a mother, but of her assertion that I was the daughter she never had. Is this how she'd treat a fucking daughter?

Streaks of fire burn my cheeks as my fists pound the door. Not until I began yelling her name and demanding she tell me where Ethan has taken my daughter, does she open up, and that's only to tell me I have five minutes to get off her property before she calls the police.

I storm away as a bolt of lightning shoots across the sky, the sudden crackle startling me and pushing out even more of the tears I was trying to hold in. Before I make it to my car, the rain starts to fall, the drops mingling with the water in my eyes as I realize I don't know what else to do or where to turn.

Desperate for anything that can determine my child's whereabouts, I drive by Ethan's new place, his job, and his friends', and either there is no sign of him or I get zero cooperation.

Back at home, the tears continue to fall. Each new surge, a hot trail of agony that burns just under my skin. A deep emptiness fills my heart as the emotions shatter and rip the seams I can no longer hold together.

And I wait.

And wait.

And wait.

My phone doesn't ring and the doorbell doesn't sound. Ethan's taken my daughter and there's not a damn thing I can do except pray he comes to his senses. Being that prayer didn't work too well for me in the past, I'm not holding out hope that it will this time either.

I haven't been to work since the day Ethan showed up with his demands and threats. Aunt Sophie called and explained everything to Jim Bob. Not that I care in the slightest about that crummy-ass job at this point.

I've barely eaten anything and what I *have* managed to swallow comes right back up. Sleep only comes when my body is too exhausted to do much more than perform involuntary functions. I go to the room I share with my daughter and straighten her things. Her toys, her coloring books, her clothes. Anything to make me feel closer to her.

And then there are the tears. I've cried so much, my ducts seem to have dried up. I lift the frame from the dresser and stare at the picture of the happy little girl swinging in the park. An ache moves through my chest as I study the smile on her face, and even though I don't know where she is, I'm hoping she's smiling. That Ethan is taking good care of her. I trace my fingers across the picture and think about the hopes and dreams I have for my child.

"I promised your life wouldn't be like mine, but it's already become the crazy epilogue of the story I thought I'd ended."

When I get my daughter back—and I will get her back, I won't accept the alternative—there will be changes. First of which is working harder to become the person I know I need to be for her.

Chapter
SIXTEEN

Branch

HEAVING SOBS RESONATE THROUGH THE PHONE. The name displayed on the screen was Loretta Perez but no way could this be her. Not the Loretta Perez I know. But I still ask, "Loretta…is that you?"

"Yes." She sniffs. "It's me."

"Has something happened to Mama or Jace?" My breath catches as I await confirmation of my worst fear.

"I'm sorry but I have horrible news. Something I still can't process."

I brace myself, prepared to hear that Mama has disappeared again or something worse—that her mental issues have hurt Jace somehow.

"It's Jimmy."

Jimmy? Speaking of which, why is Loretta calling me instead of him?

Another sniff.

"Jimmy is…is…" She falls silent, as if she's choking back

more tears.

I hold the phone as the hairs on my neck stand up.

"My Jimmy is in heaven with his mama," she finally gets it out.

Her words cycle back through my head. "I couldn't have heard you right."

She breaks down, crying convulsively, the sobs mingled with the sound of struggles to breathe against the cries. "He's gone, Branch. My Jimmy is gone."

"Loretta, what happened?"

"He passed away in his garage. He'd been working late on a car he wanted to get to a customer the following morning. I was driving home after a trip to the grocery store and decided to stop by to tell him the work day was over and I wanted him home with me."

Before she can finish, she's overcome with emotion. I hold the line—already numb by news I can't seem to wrap my head around. After she composes herself enough to go on, she says, "Everything was quiet when I walked in. Too quiet. And then I saw his feet. He'd been—"

Her words are cut off when the deep sobs resurface. And again, when she's restored a margin of calm, she continues. "He'd been trapped underneath the car. I called 911, but it was already too late. His body was almost completely severed. He'd been lying there for hours."

I fall back, stumbling and dropping in the chair closest to me. My body lax. My mind racing. "No. Not Jimmy," I mumble.

"I can't believe it either. I keep telling myself this is some horrible nightmare and I'm gonna wake up and Jimmy will be walking in the door ready to tell me some new story about how he knows I'm carrying a boy this time. And the girls… they're devastated. Jimmy was the world to those kids."

"And to you."

"Yes…and to me."

And to me.

"I'm trying my best to keep it together. But I don't know how to exist without him. I just don't. He's all I know."

I'm silent. Staring straight ahead, my eyes glazed over. I swallow the words I need to say and just listen, but the line is quiet. And then Loretta starts to cry again. She needs to hear words of comfort. She needs to know that it will be okay. But how the fuck can it *ever* be okay? Do I lie and tell her what I know isn't true? No, I can't do that. But what I *can* tell her is that she has friends and family who will be there, to help her through this but silence holds my tongue. I'm flooded with memories of Jimmy, of the lessons I've learned, of the talks that kept me sane at a time when Mama had driven me to the brink…of my acceptance of his role as my honorary father without my ever actually saying the words aloud. That's what's between Loretta and me. *Memories.* Those that belong to her and Jimmy, those that another soul will never know, those that will remain forever in her heart. I need to tell her that. That Jimmy will always be with her. That he is in their kids…in their unborn child, but I say nothing. I hear Loretta crying, and the words still don't come. *Jimmy Perez. No longer in this world?* The thought alone is so fucked that I can't imagine the reality.

Almost robotically, I ask, "Have you made any arrangements? For a service?"

"Yes, that's why I'm calling. I'm meeting with the pastor and his wife this evening and they're gonna help with the planning. I'm in the hospital."

"Is it the baby?"

"Yeah. My blood pressure shot through the roof and now I have something called preeclampsia, so they're taking precautions."

"And the kids. Where are they?"

"My aunt is here and my sister is flying in tomorrow or the next day. I can't remember what she said, to be honest."

I stand, then pace back and forth between the window and the TV. "Is there anything I can do?"

"Just be here. You're family and having you close will feel as though another part of Jimmy is here with me. I need that right now."

This doesn't seem right. Jimmy can't be dead. No fucking way.

"Branch?"

"Yes. I'm still here. I'm just…I don't know."

"Umm. The service will be later this week. Thursday."

"I'll be there, Loretta. Anything else you need, just let me know."

"Thanks, Branch. I will."

"And call anytime."

The call drops and so does the air from my lungs. I stand in place, my fingers curved around the phone. A burning in my chest courses through my frame and I explode with rage. My phone flies across the room, shattering the eighty-eight-inch screen TV, then falling to the floor and breaking into scattered pieces.

I place the glass on the bar and reach for the bottle of Macallan.

I've had this one for a while.

Was saving it for a special occasion.

When Jimmy told me he thought they were finally going to have the boy he wanted, I decided *that* would be the occasion. To drink it with Jimmy and celebrate the birth of his fifth child. His boy.

I look at the bottle, turning it over in my hands before finally deciding to open it. Foregoing a glass, I bring the bottle to my lips and swallow, the sting of the whiskey burning on its way down.

How can Jimmy be gone?

I walk toward the window that spans the side of the room and stare out into the Dallas night. Tears burn the back of my eyes, but not being one to cry, I bring the whiskey to my lips and as if the bottle were an untapped spigot, I pour the alcohol down my throat. If I'm taking it this bad, Loretta and the kids are barely holding on.

For the next hour, I sit in this spot, beside the window, my vision blurred as I lose myself in the bottle of whiskey.

I'm drunk as shit but it does nothing to dull the gravity of loss. With a grimace, I polish off the remainder of the alcohol, then grunt as I pull myself up from the floor and stagger to the bedroom.

I need to get back to Georgia. To be there for Jimmy's family like he was there for me. I don't know how to begin to step into his shoes. Jimmy always knew the right thing to say. He knew when it was best to say nothing at all, to let you figure things out on your own. Can I be that person for five kids? And a widow? Shit, I can barely do right by Mama and Jace.

Jimmy would tell me I'll be exactly who and what they need when the situation presents itself—that all I'll need to do is follow my gut. So that's what I'll have to do. When the time comes, I'll follow my gut. For now, I have to prepare myself to bury a man who was more like a father. A man who was my best friend.

I awake on the floor next to the wall of windows. An empty bottle of whiskey and a brunette are my companions. I squint at the light pouring into the room, a million tiny hammers pounding in my head as I try to retrieve the events of last night. But when it all comes crashing into my mind's eye, a tsunami of grief rolls through me. I deploy the methods I've used in the past to quieten emotions I don't particularly care for, but this I can't control.

I look up at the ceiling, remembering the phone call. Loretta's voice. Her sobs. And my inability to comfort her. And then there was my cell and the shattered TV screen.

After my rendezvous with the first bottle of whiskey, I grabbed my tablet and FaceTimed Connie, telling her I needed a replacement phone and a flight to Georgia. Then I asked her for something else. And since there's a naked woman lying inches away from me, she obviously delivered.

I scan the span of the space around me. The upscale penthouse. The expensive furnishings. *The Branch McGuire Wall of Fame.* The brunette on the floor. And the empty bottle of liquor.

It all twists like acid in my gut, and suddenly everything I thought I wanted becomes everything I need to escape. What the fuck have I been doing? The total disregard for anything significant. The random women. The lack of connections—something I suddenly feel desperate for. Someone to hold. Someone who will understand. Someone I can drown myself in.

But there isn't anyone.

I think of Connie and Vaughn. I think of my teammates. Then I think of the people in Blue Ridge—Mama, Dad, and my high school buddies. I cycle through the haze of images running through my head until one slows with laser-sharp focus.

Ragan.

Chapter
SEVENTEEN

Ragan

I START TO WAKE UP.

It feels like I'm lying in a sauna and it takes my breath. I swallow and wipe the back of my hand over my forehead. My skin is clammy and my throat is parched.

With exaggerated effort, my lids flutter open, bringing the patterned markings on the ceiling into focus.

Movement in the corner of the bedroom pulls my attention toward the door, and my gaze falls upon Aunt Sophie sitting in the chair across from me.

With a groan, I push myself up and peel back the layer of blankets.

"How are you feeling?" she asks.

I look at her, disoriented. "What's going on?"

"You fainted."

I don't remember anything.

"When's the last time you've eaten?"

For the first time in as long as I can remember, she looks

at me with kind eyes. Her short dishwater-blond hair, accented with graying curls, falls on either side of her slim face and a sweet smile spreads over her thin lips. It's still oddly peculiar to see concern in her expression, especially in relation to me. "I don't remember." I move to get out of bed.

"Stay put. I've made stew. I'll bring you a bowl."

As I start to gather my wits, I realize it's been a week and I've heard nothing. I have absolutely no idea where my daughter is, if she's okay or if I'll ever see her again. How can anyone elicit this type of mental anguish on another human being? *How*?

Hayley has been with me nearly every day—Channing Tatum in tow. She's afraid to leave him alone because his condition is deteriorating. I couldn't bring myself to tell Noah. I've actually avoided his calls, only replying in text that I'm crazy exhausted from work and we'll catch up when things settle down. The last thing I need is for him to come here and land himself in trouble. Carrie has stopped by, called or texted her prayers that CeeCee will be home soon. Dad, Uncle Stan and even Aunt Sophie have surrounded me with support and kindness. But I see the worry in their eyes deepen with each passing day.

Each swallow of Aunt Sophie's stew is like dropping a coin into a well with no bottom—I'm on empty, both emotionally and physically. I take in as much as I can before that same sick feeling that's kept me bent over the toilet resurfaces.

After sitting still for a while in hopes the food stays down, I decide to shower the past several days' worth of grime away. Setting the temperature of the water as hot as my skin can tolerate it, I stand beneath the shower head and let it spray over me. The cyclic heaves from continuously throwing up over the last several days have left a tender ache in my belly. And now as I start to cry, my body shakes and prods those sore muscles.

When the water starts to run cold, I slip out of the shower and grab a towel to dry myself and another for my hair. I could actually go back to sleep—anything to make me forget what's going on. Instead, I pull on a pair of jeans, noticing how loose they are but taking no joy in the obvious weight loss. I grab a sweatshirt from the pile of clothes I've yet to fold and pull it on before unwrapping the towel from my hair and throwing the partially dry heap into a scraggly pony-tail. I check my phone—on the off-chance Ethan has finally grown a conscience but there aren't any calls from him. Just a text from Carrie saying she's praying for Cecelia's safe return.

Stepping into the hallway, I head to the living room when I hear Aunt Sophie exclaim, "Oh, thank heavens. Ragan, come quick. Hurry." With my heart in my chest, I run toward the voices and see my smiling little girl in Dad's arms.

A flood of relief rushes through me as tears spring to my eyes and my heart finally starts to beat at its correct rhythm.

"Mommy," my daughter yells. Dad passes her to me and I pull her into a hug, so caught up in her that I don't bother to notice that Ethan isn't in the room.

Chapter
EIGHTEEN

Ragan

THE NEXT THIRTY-SIX HOURS ARE SPENT SOAKING UP every second I can with my daughter before falling back into my routine. What I really want to do is grab CeeCee and our few belongings, hop in my car and just drive. Placing everything about Blue Ridge where it belongs…behind me.

As for the father of my child, not only had he taken my daughter in the most underhanded and despicable way, he returned her home in much the same manner. My little girl was standing at the front door *alone* while my worthless ex sat in his Jeep waiting for her to ring the bell. And when Dad answered and scooped his grandchild into his arms, Ethan pulled off without a word.

For the thousands of heartbeats that throbbed in my chest and the hundreds of breaths I struggled to catch, for the countless tear drops that soaked my pillow and the millions of seconds that fear inhabited every cell in my body, he excused it all with a letter. A half-page of his messy script explaining that our daughter's happiness was the most important thing in the world to him, even it that happiness meant bringing her home when she asked. That's how that bastard ended seven days of misery—with a fucking letter!

I'm not stupid. He didn't bring CeeCee back to me because he valued her happiness. The only reason he brought her home is because he's ill-equipped to care for a toddler. Taking my daughter was nothing more than a power play. To show me he has the upper hand and he'll use it whenever he wants.

I fight to drown the emotions that will most assuredly ruin my day, then busy myself with cleaning the tables in my station, more thankful than ever for the generous tips from the regulars. Since a court order is the only way to protect my daughter, every extra dime is going toward legal fees. Of course, that means working more hours, which unfortunately means less time with CeeCee, but what choice do I have?

I tuck the few bucks in my pocket and whirl around just as the chatter in the diner increases an octave, a knot forming in my throat when I discover the cause.

"What are you doing here?" I ask, my brows furrow as Branch comes to a stop a few feet in front of me. "I thought we agreed to stay away from each other."

"We did."

"Then why are you here?" Is it because of the fight with Ethan? Or the night we'd had sex? Either way, he shouldn't be here.

"Did you hear about Jimmy?"

I stare at him, confused. He looks different...tired. Like

he hasn't slept in days. His eyes are bloodshot and the bill of his hat is pulled low over his face, as if he's hiding what he doesn't want the world to see. "No, I haven't heard anything. Or even seen him since the day on the lake." *Not to mention, I've had my own stuff to deal with.*

He looks as if the mention of Lake Blue Ridge is a memory he'd rather forget. "I'm in town for his funeral."

"What? No!" I reply, a palm covering my gasp. "What happened?"

For a split second, sadness clouds his features and then it appears he chokes back a surge of emotion. When my customer beckons for her check, I ask Carrie to cover for me as I step to the breakroom to speak with Branch in private.

At the back door of the diner, Branch shifts his feet, lets out a sigh and says, "I know he really liked you, so does Loretta. So I figured you'd want to know."

I liked Jimmy, too…and his wife. They seemed as if they were the perfect couple. "I'm so sorry." I didn't know Jimmy very well, but I knew he meant a great deal to Branch.

He leans against the door, exhaling his grief as he looks up at the ceiling. "I just can't believe he's gone, you know."

I reach out to him, my hand settling softly on his forearm. "Is there anything I can do?"

Branch meets my eyes. He looks lost, as if he isn't sure what he needs or who can give it to him.

"Will you go for a ride with me?"

"Er…sure. I guess."

"I'm not ready to face Loretta and the girls just yet. And I'm not ready to be around anyone who *really* knew Jimmy. Not right now."

"Okay. So where would you like to go?"

"Anywhere."

I still have another half hour before my shift ends and I honestly don't think I'm the best choice of distractions, but I don't have the heart to tell him that.

"I'm here for another thirty minutes."

"I'll wait."

Before we exit the diner, Branch purchases a few bottles of beer, then we walk out to a huge black SUV—not the red Corvette he usually drives. We end up at a typical modern-styled house that looks to be abandoned. From the outside, it appears to equal the size of Dad's place but with a perfectly manicured—although yellowed—lawn and everything in its rightful place, as if it's for sale but missing the realtor's signage.

Branch and I walk up the drive, only awkwardness between us, and sit on the front steps. After a period of silence, he starts to talk. About nothing in particular. Just arbitrary things. I suspect this is his way of overshadowing the space in his head he isn't ready to deal with.

Our conversation wavers from general to personal, then back to general again. He eventually tells me we're sitting on the steps of a house he owns—the one he grew up in. Each time he visits Blue Ridge, he stops by and sits on the steps. Sometimes he lounges in the porch swing but that's as far as he goes. Although it's fully furnished, he never steps a foot inside.

I don't ask why. I figure he doesn't want me to know.

Though I'm curious, I won't push. I'm still not sure why he sought me out. But I don't say that, either. Instead, I listen and chime in when there is a lull in the conversation. When it appears he's run out of random topics, I decide on a safe one—or at least one I hope doesn't dredge up any sadness.

"What would you be doing if you weren't a football player? Or have you ever thought along those lines?"

"I haven't. Not once. I love the game. I don't know who I am without it."

"You're pretty amazing. I could literally watch you play all day."

Branch arches a brow and chuckles. "You could, huh?"

"Did I say something funny?"

He passes a bottle of beer to me. "Thought you didn't like football?"

I nudge his leg with mine, pursing my lips to hide my smile. "Okay, so I lied. I would have said anything to be in opposition of you."

A smile slants the corner of his mouth. He knows as well as I do that he was a freaking jerk. He downs the last of his beer and looks out across the yard.

Well, since he's here and in obvious need of a diversion, I figure I can ask something I've often wondered. "The way you play. It seems as natural as breathing for you. Is it?"

He twists the cap off a fresh beer, taps the neck of it against mine and takes a long pull. "Everyone seems to thinks so."

"But that's not true?"

He chews the inside of his cheek for a moment, as if he's considering how to best explain to me. "Most times it feels that way...like it's an extension of me. I know that sounds crazy, but when I step onto the field, everything just clicks.

It's like the world makes sense and the sole purpose for my existence is to play. I mean, I actually feel it the second it happens—it's as if something that was lying dormant wakes up and takes over. I can read the players, predict their moves. Like someone is on my shoulder whispering it all to me."

I stare at him, easily recalling the plays where he effortlessly threw a pass, the ball soaring through the air as if it had taken flight. Or when he ran down the field himself, maneuvering through defensive lines without so much as a single touch by the opposing team, even when they were directly in his path. The only explanation is that it's a gift. An innate talent.

"Wow."

"Some people have to work at something for years that comes so easy for me. When I first realized I was pretty good, it was all I could think about. I couldn't get enough of it. Being good at something makes it easy to love, I guess."

"And that's how it's always been, something that makes a part of you come alive?"

A grimace mars his expression. "Not exactly. There was a time when football became less of a love affair and more of an escape. Back then it was from the fights at home, and some years later from the guilt of leaving Mama and Jace in Blue Ridge."

Branch sets the empty bottle on the step in the space between us. I watch the emotions he doesn't want to show play out on his face. I don't say anything because I sense this is a difficult topic for him and he'll say more when he's ready.

"It fucks with my head a lot. Leaving them behind." He looks down, and reaches for the bill of his hat, pulling it lower over his face. "I guess it wouldn't have if Mama had somehow moved on with her life. But she never really did, she swayed back and forth for years. And it was all centered around my dad." A cynical laugh escapes his lips. "And I resent the fuck out of that guy…probably more than I should," he adds. "He could have made it easier for us back then."

"But you two seemed fine when we had dinner at Jim—" The plan was to distract him but here I am bringing it up again.

"Yep, we'd just reconnected actually. Before then, it was radio silence. He was right here in Blue Ridge but he may as well have been hundreds of miles away. He was one of those classic absentee parents. I didn't really accept that until one day when I was Jace's age."

"Why then? Did something happen?"

"More like *didn't* happen. Although he and Mama weren't together and were constantly at each other's throats, he still came around from time to time. And of all the days I waited on him to show up, there's one that's as clear in my mind as if it happened yesterday."

I take a look over my shoulder at the porch that's perfectly staged to attract perspective buyers—two wooden rockers, large planters and an eye-catching wind chime. Then I glance at the front yard—the flower beds and the picket fence, and try to imagine Branch's life here. It only makes me that much more curious as to why he'd visit a place for which he obviously harbors ill feelings.

"What happened?"

Branch leans forward, propping his elbows on his knees, his gaze still cast downward. "We had a day planned…to go fishing. Like any boy anxious to spend time with his father, I was excited. I even ditched my friends that day, just to be with him. I packed a lunch, came out to this very step, and waited for hours. Mama came out every few minutes to persuade me inside, saying he wasn't going to show up, that he was *never* going to show up for anything anymore. I mean, she raked him over the coals every chance she could. But I refused to believe her. So I waited. And waited. I ended up eating every bit of that lunch I'd packed as I sat here…waiting. The sun went down. And I was still here. But he never fucking came."

He doesn't say anything further. He just shakes his head and exhales a breath.

Say something, Ragan. Okay, but what? I can pop off the quick comebacks when he's the asshat ball player whose every word is loaded with innuendo. But when he's just a regular guy carrying on a regular conversation about something so personal, and obviously painful, I react as if I'm shell-shocked. "I hate that happened to you. No child should ever experience that type of disappointment."

Branch lifts his Redhorns hat, runs a hand through his hair, and then flips the cap to the back. "If you love someone, if you *really* love someone, why would you do that? Why would you ever leave them waiting like that?"

His words squeeze my heart and I want to say the right thing, anything to give him an answer to a question I really can't answer, but I sense his question is more to himself than to me, so I don't reply. When I see he isn't going to say more, I reach out and touch his hand, hoping it offers some semblance of comfort. "I'm sorry. I know firsthand about men who suck at fatherhood," I say, thinking of Ethan and my own dad.

"Mama was great though, in some ways."

"How so?"

"She was always there for me. As much as she could be anyway. Trying to fill in some of the gaps, encouraging me to excel in school…hence the degree in Communications and Business. Mama wasn't too keen on the football thing back then," he replies in response to my raised brows. "She was somewhat of a nature enthusiast, so when she was up to it, we had scavenger hunts in the park. We played a lot of games, too. There was one called dots and boxes that I remember playing when I was in grade school."

"I don't think I've ever heard of that."

"It's just some silly paper game, connecting adjacent dots on a piece of paper until one player is able to form a square. We'd write an initial in the square, and in the end, the person with the most squares was the winner."

"Interesting."

"I guess. She'd make a game out of just about anything. As a matter of fact, there was one time when there was literally no food in the house. And she even made that into a game—she said it was a scavenger hunt for spare change. We searched under sofa cushions, in junk drawers, under the bed—you name it, we searched it. We scrounged up enough to buy a jar of peanut butter and a loaf of bread. A dollar shy of adding a jar of jelly, though. But she made that into a game, too. To see how many bites we could swallow without a sip of water. She had a way of putting a spin on everything to make it seem like it was something great."

I smile at his euphoric expression. "Sounds like she loved you very much."

"Yeah. It does, doesn't it?"

"At least from where I'm sitting."

He nods, turns away from my inquisitive eyes and vanishes somewhere inside his head. "She's a schizophrenic." The words come soft, almost as if he was saying it to himself.

I didn't expect that. Then again, I didn't expect to ever see Branch again, unless it was on TV.

"She was always a little quirky but it got worse over the years."

"Were there problems with her medication? I know that can often be an issue."

"We didn't know of her diagnosis back then so she wasn't on meds. But her turn for the worse was more than likely a result of some marijuana that had been laced with something."

"That sounds pretty horrible."

Yep. And it was supplied to her by none other than Dad himself."

"Your dad?"

"Yeah, but that's a whole other story."

"I didn't know drugs could do that. I thought schizophrenia was caused by a genetic physiological imbalance."

"It can be. But the use of drugs that affect the mind and mental functioning has been linked to schizophrenia. So the consensus is that psychoactive drugs like marijuana trigger symptoms in those who are susceptible."

"I'm so sorry, Branch. That couldn't have been easy for someone so young. Losing your dad and caring for your mother."

He shrugs. "She's my mama. Did what I had to do. She couldn't hold down a job and Dad wasn't the model payer of child support—or so I'd been led to believe but that's another story, too. I've got lots of 'em. Anyway, I knew I needed to help, so I started working at Jimmy's Garage. I used the money to chip in on the bills and then later to help out with my kid brother when he came along."

"That was very noble, Branch. Most kids would have been all about themselves."

"Don't applaud me for that. I can be a bit of a selfish asshole."

I smile in silent agreement.

"Not disputing that one, huh?" he asks. "I'm the stereotypical ball player but I guess you've figured that out already."

"From a glimpse, it appears that way. But if you give anyone half a chance to take a closer look—which I don't think you ever do—they'll see what I'm starting to see. That there's more to you than stats, arrogance, money, and bedding women. You're not the stereotype. Well, at least not below the surface. I think you hide behind all of that superficial crap because it's easier than taking a chance on someone."

He throws me an inquisitive look. "Why would I want to do something stupid like that?"

"It's not stupid and you know it. But it's pretty clear you won't allow yourself to see it any other way. From the sound of it, you're letting everything in your past dictate your present."

He looks at me as if I've uncovered something he'd rather keep hidden.

"Everyone won't leave you high and dry, Branch."

"If the ones who are most important in your life do exactly that, then it stands to reason that others who are of lesser importance will do the same damn thing," he replies, his tone bitter.

"So because of what you *think*, which is insane by the

way, your plan is to keep doing as you have—going from city to city and titty to titty? Is that what you really want out of life? Foregoing meaningful connections. Fucking random women. Never giving yourself a chance to grow or to find that *one*?"

He looks away, diverting his eyes from mine. "Who needs *the one*? Besides I love tits," he adds with a grin.

He's deflecting and the door he'd cracked open is starting to close. But for those fleeting moments, he was more relatable, almost comforting, when he slipped from behind the façade. But having sensed his discomfort with this topic, I change the subject. "How are things with your mom now? Better?"

"For the most part. Up until recently she was still holding onto her resentment of dad. I'm talking years and years of lies and hatred, but now they can't seem to stay away from each other. She's actually doing better than her doctor predicted. And as much as I hate to admit it, it's partially due to Dad." He shakes his head in disbelief. "It's all just crazy."

"Why did they break up?"

"I honestly think it goes back to before they even met. Mama had dreams of attending Julliard."

"That's the Performing Arts School in New York, right?"

"Yeah."

"Oh, wow. Incredible school."

"She loves the arts. Especially dance. My grandparents had her in performing art camps every summer and in a few other programs pretty much year round since she was six years old. So from early on, that was the plan for her life. She wanted to be on Broadway."

"That's some dream."

"Yeah. But she met and fell in love with my dad. Let go of her dream to follow his. They moved to Atlanta when he was drafted to play with the Seahawks. Six months later, she was pregnant with me and they decided to marry. A year later, Dad had a shoulder injury that wrecked it all. We later ended up in Blue Ridge for a coaching job Dad wanted but that only lasted for about two years. After that he had a few random jobs that didn't pay much, so money was tight. The fights started around that time. Mama throwing Dad's failures in his face and blaming him for stealing her dreams."

"That's sad. That she didn't get to do something she was so passionate about."

"Yeah. That's why I tried to give something back to her, so to speak. Like you, she loves fine art. A few years back, I surprised Mama with a dream house full of it—paintings, sculptures, music on vinyl—the whole nine yards. As a matter of fact, you can drop by sometime and I'll show you the pieces we have."

"I'd love to see them. Thank you."

"No problem. A fan owns a gallery in New York, and he selected everything. Actually, his 'art tutorials' are what enabled me to pick up on how good you are."

"Hmm. I wouldn't expect you to be the artsy type."

"And you'd be right. Not that I asked him but I guess creative types like to share the knowledge. I didn't really care to hear it—I just wanted something Mama would like. I have a couple of pieces at my penthouse in Dallas, too."

"Are you *sure* you're not an in-the-closet art connoisseur?"

He chuckles. "Positive. I had very little to do with most of the stuff in my place. Connie had someone come in and do it all. I only had a couple of requests—my TV and the *Branch*

McGuire Wall of Fame."

"Why am I not surprised?"

"It's just some sports memorabilia I've collected over the years."

"I'm sure it's Branch McGuire at his finest."

"You think?"

"With an ego like yours…I *know*."

His lips curve into a smile. "Maybe."

"So back to my original question, why did your parents split?"

"In a nutshell—Dad's career. It didn't pan out the way they'd hoped and that led to endless fights about money. That was always a daily topic in the McGuire household. Drove me fucking crazy. I guess that's why I always wanted so much money of my own. I didn't want to worry about that shit. And I definitely didn't want a woman looking over my shoulder undermining and nagging the hell out of me."

My brows furrow. "Is that how you see your mom?"

"I see many sides of her."

"Oh," I say, and scan his face, trying to figure out why he has such a wide range of views of his mom.

He doesn't say anything for a measure.

"I sense you don't like my description of the person who brought me into this world."

I shrug. "You have your reasons. We all do."

"Mama kept a lot of secrets. And she manipulated me a lot. She still does. Maybe it's my fault for letting her get away with it. I wanted to make her happy. I wanted things to be a little easier for her."

"Sounds like you had to be strong at a time when that strength should have come from a parent."

"I guess you're right. You know, ever since I can remember, I had to be strong for everyone. Mama, Jace, myself. I've never had the chance to break. I think everyone deserves that."

Something else I can relate to.

We fall into a different kind of silence. It's comfortable. And it feels...nice. Despite the grim circumstance that brought us here, when I glance at him now, he looks unburdened. Perhaps that means he can now face what he wasn't ready to.

I take a sip of beer and lean against the railing. It occurs to me that this is the most at ease I've felt since Branch walked into the diner hours ago. But that lightheartedness instantly fades when he looks at me and asks, "So what's *your* story?"

Chapter
NINETEEN

Ragan

"N̲O̲T̲ ̲S̲U̲R̲E̲ ̲Y̲O̲U̲ ̲R̲E̲A̲L̲L̲Y̲ ̲W̲A̲N̲T̲ ̲T̲O̲ ̲H̲E̲A̲R̲ ̲M̲Y̲ story."

He brushes his shoulder against mine, an innocent gesture that somersaults my insides. "You listened to mine."

"Yeah but I didn't know we were trading tales of woe." Though I never shared this part of myself with anyone besides Ethan and Hayley, I find myself wanting to open up to Branch. I take a breath and step into the shadows of my past. "A year after giving birth to my brother, my mother ran off. Abandoned Noah and me and never looked back."

His eyes widen, and once he's given my words a chance to sink in, he asks, "Who does shit like that?"

"Oh, let me finish. It gets better. My mom's an addict and she used drugs the entire time she carried me. So yeah, I was what they called a crack baby." I look down at my feet and scrape the toe of my shoe over the pebble on the step.

"Luckily Dad was around to keep it at bay, so I wasn't born with any type of addiction, just a shitload of immune issues. Three years later, she had Noah. A year after that she was gone. She left for work one Friday morning and never returned. She finally had the gumption to call a month after and tell Dad she wasn't coming back."

I hesitantly look up at Branch and then relax when I see his blue gaze soft with sympathy. "That's pretty fucked. Do you know where she is now?"

I shrug. "Who gives a shit? Last I heard, she was in jail."

His heavy brows furrow in question to my statement.

"Shoplifting. Prostitution. Drugs. Those are her usual three."

"What about her side of the family? I would guess she stays in contact with them."

"I wouldn't know. Dad doesn't talk about them anymore and I don't use my real last name on social media because I don't want them to know shit about me. The only reason I know about her bouts with the law is because when I was younger I tried to find her and saw details of her arrests in the online newspaper."

"And now you're no longer curious?"

"Not really. They knew what my life was like and never tried to help so to hell with them."

He nods. "I get that, I guess."

"And the one relative I did manage to find on Facebook basically blew me off, so I decided I was on my own."

His eyes roam over my face. "So your dad raised you?"

"I wouldn't exactly say that."

"What *would* you say?"

"I pretty much raised myself."

"So…there's more to your story?"

I hesitate for a moment, wondering if I should tell him the rest. "Yeah. A lot more. A year or so after Mom left, Dad married Cassidy Merritt, the woman who gave *evil stepmother* a new face."

"That doesn't sound too good."

"It was fucking horrible. She had two kids of her own and since we had the larger home, they all moved in with us. And that's when her true colors started to show." I take a deep breath and push down the emotion that rises in my chest. "For a while she was nice, but then she was only nice in front of Dad and eventually she didn't bother trying at all."

"So she was one of those classic mean-just-for-the-hell-of-it stepmothers?"

"*Mean?* I would have taken mean any day. She beat the shit out of us for everything except breathing…and Dad let her."

As the shock registers on his face, I offer him a smile. Even though I know he sees the pain behind it.

"Ragan…"

I shake my head. "Don't."

His eyes skate over my face and he gives me that look, the same woeful expression I saw on Hayley's face when I finally told her. I turn away and bring the bottle of beer to my lips, then I apply the mask that covers it all—the one I've hidden behind for most of my life. After a long exhale, I tell him the rest.

"Two months before graduation, shit hit the fan. I finally stood up to her and she kicked me out with the clothes on my back and a small grocery bag of stuff I'd managed to grab before the door locked behind me."

"And your dad let all this shit happen?"

"Yup."

"Now it all makes sense, the awkwardness I saw when I was at your place." He shakes his head.

Another reaction that mimics Hayley's.

"So after I left, I knew I had to find some way to check on Noah, make sure he was okay. They wouldn't let me in the house, so I went to the school. I don't know how, but Cassidy found out. And the next time I dropped by his class, Noah told me I had to stay away because he'd get a beating if I didn't. So that's what I did…I stayed away, thinking it would keep him safe. Then one day out of the blue, he messages me on Facebook saying he was running away. And he literally disappeared. I never heard anything from him until a couple of weeks ago."

His bemused expression meets the long-suffering of mine.

"It's okay. You don't have to say anything," I murmur. "This story would leave anyone speechless."

No words are spoken for several long minutes, then he finally asks, "How's your brother? It must have been a relief to finally reconnect."

I'm suddenly smiling, thinking fondly of Noah. "Yes, it was. He's great. Living in Washington. Engaged, successful, adopted by an amazing family."

"That's pretty cool. Any plans to move closer to him?"

"I'd love that. He actually suggested it, but my ex, he'll make it next to impossible."

"That guy is a fucking prick," Branch spits out, his lips curling into a grimace.

"Yeah. He is." I think about CeeCee and the torture her

asshole of a father inflicted upon us. My eyes water at the memory of those frantic days without my precious baby girl. I go on to tell Branch about the hell Ethan put me through when he'd taken my daughter. I see the anger flash in Branch's eyes and recall his fight with Ethan. Then I think about how CeeCee and Branch had instantly hit it off. He genuinely has a soft spot for my little angel.

And that's it. We don't say anything more about it. We prop against opposite sides of the steps and stare out across the lawn. I guess we're both thinking about the stories we shared. And I sense neither of us plans to say anything further about our shattered beginnings.

"Can I ask you a question and get an honest answer?" Branch asks sometime later as we head to the car.

I can already sense his question is one I don't want to answer, but I nod anyway. "Sure."

"When I was last in town, Chad told me something really odd about you."

Oh shit. He *did* recognize me.

"He says he ran into you at a Greek restaurant in Mountain Park."

"Well, he lied," I reply, almost too abruptly.

"Why would he do that?"

"Am I supposed to be a mind reader? Who knows why people do anything?"

"Okay, so maybe he didn't run into you, but he said he saw you hanging out with some dude and it looked like a date."

"And? People go on dates all the time." *Oh, God. Please let him drop this.*

We reach the SUV, Branch stands near the driver's side

as he holds my gaze. "He said the lighting was kinda low but he was pretty sure it was you. And you were sitting at a table with some bald guy who looked old enough to be your dad."

Chad was the guy I'd caught staring at me that night. I should have known that evening would come back to haunt me.

Branch looks unsure if he should finish. But he does. And I feel as if I want to disappear. "He said right there at the table—where anyone could have seen—you pulled off your panties and passed them to that guy. But when you looked up and saw Chad watching, you grabbed the underwear and ran out of the restaurant."

I let out a nervous laugh. "Does that even sound like something anyone in their right mind would do?"

"Well…no. But you don't really fit into that category."

"Why? Because I'm not crawling all over you?"

"Well, that is *one* reason." He smirks and then turns all serious. "Did that really happen?"

As suspected, it's a question I don't want to answer. But I do, in a roundabout way. "Haven't you ever fallen on hard times and done things you knew you wouldn't otherwise?"

He nods, realizing that what his friend told him was the truth.

"I have a kid and I needed money to pay for childcare. Found that guy's ad on Craigslist about buying used panties for three hundred dollars a pair, so I decided to do it. But when I saw Chad watching me, I realized how far I'd fallen so I snatched my underwear from that freak and ran off. The next day, I moved out of Hayley's parents' place."

"And back to your dad's?"

I frown and roll my eyes. "Yeah, but it's temporary. I

hate walking into that house. Being there buries me in every memory I ran away from. The endless abuse. The lack of protection. I can never forgive Dad for not being a real father to me, so living with him brings up a lot of negative feelings and even more nightmares. Neither of which I want around my daughter. But hey, for now that's the best I can do."

Branch nods again. And I know he understands. He went through hard times growing up himself but he's in a better place now. I let out a sigh and look past him, staring into the distance and envisioning myself in a better place, too. "Unless I get that used panty business going. There's always that."

We break out in laughter and slide into the SUV.

I buckle in and look over at Branch. He's still smiling. Hmm. Branch McGuire is actually pretty cool to hang out with. Who knew?

Chapter
TWENTY

Ragan

"T HANKS, RAGAN."

"For what?"

"Being the friend I don't deserve," he says. And this time there's no trace of humor in his expression. Branch McGuire is being sincere.

"If there's anything I can do, promise you'll ask."

He nods, then pulls his phone from his pocket to check the incoming text. "Looks like Loretta's home from the hospital. I'm going to head over to Jim—head over to check on her. I've put it off long enough."

"Aunt Sophie has CeeCee, so how about I tag along with you?" I ask, sensing he needs me there but knowing he won't admit that he does. "I'd like to pay my respects. And I'm sure Loretta can use all the help she can get with the girls right now."

An older lady with an apron at her waist and her hair pulled up and away from her face greets us at the door. After observing her interaction with Branch, I realize she's Loretta's Aunt Isabella. She tells us that Loretta is on a call with the minister who'll be officiating the funeral.

I immediately feel the heartache that saturates the air around us, the weight of the sadness heavy as we move further into the house.

The girls run to Branch when we enter the living room. He lifts Tess in one arm and wraps the other around Isadora.

A smile whispers at the edges of Loretta's mouth as she looks at the five of them. She then smooths a palm over her belly and gestures for me to take a seat beside her on the sofa. I give her a hug and offer my condolences. I also offer my help with her daughters. To my surprise, she accepts, saying the girls need their school assignments and possibly help with their homework. She also mentions her aunt can use some assistance with grocery shopping. I use that as my excuse to give Loretta some time alone with Branch, asking the girls to help me check the pantry and the fridge so I can make a list of what I'll need to pick up.

With a couple of well-timed jokes, I manage to draw the girls into a few smiles, even if they are short-lived. After the list—which looks to primarily consist of items I'm sure they don't normally purchase—is complete, we file into the living room to find Branch and Loretta thumbing through some papers from an accordion style file box. The girls assemble on the floor around Loretta, not one of them saying a word.

I scan the grief-stricken face of each of them and my heart bleeds. The Perez household is absent of the vivacious energy it once held. That exuberance is now silence, red eyes and tearstains. I never had a father like Jimmy so when I left my dad so many years ago, I only felt relief. I can't begin to imagine what these young girls are going through having lost someone as nurturing and loving as Jimmy.

Branch and Loretta finish the business of whatever they were looking over, then Branch lifts his eyes to mine. His expression suggests he's been slapped with even more unexpected news. I wonder what was in those papers.

Branch and I sit and listen to Loretta and her daughters recite stories about Jimmy. Loretta tells us how she and Jimmy met, how he relentlessly pursued her and swore that she would one day have his babies. The girls talk about the family dinners, the days on the lake, and the game nights that Jimmy loved so much. Branch chimes in but only in brief. He primarily gazes at the five people Jimmy has left behind, an unsettling expression written over his face.

Loretta is holding up better than I expected. Had I been in her shoes—the love of my life gone, four kids and one on the way—it's safe to say I'd be an absolute wreck. When she grows tired, Loretta tells Branch she'll see him in the morning, and after the girls give us hugs, they follow her to the bedroom. Branch gives Isabella his number and tells her to call if Loretta or the girls need anything.

The drive from the Perez's house is sprinkled with music and off-topic conversation. There's no mention of Jimmy, Loretta, or the funeral. When Branch pulls to a stop in my driveway, he turns off the ignition.

"Do you work tomorrow?" he asks.

"No. Why?"

"I want to take you someplace."

"Where?"

"You'll see when we get there. Be ready at noon."

I frown.

"What is it?"

"I don't like surprises."

"And I'm not accustomed to people saying no to me."

"Well, maybe you should get accustomed to it because it will feel *especially* gratifying when they finally say yes."

He lets out an exasperated sigh.

Regardless of what he's accustomed to, I'd still say no if I didn't think I was in some way helping him cope with his grief. And although he hasn't come right out and said it, I know that I am. It's etched on his beautiful face. It's reflected in the muted blue of his eyes. It's something he can't hide—that vulnerability slipping from beneath his picture-perfect façade.

Earlier, I wondered "why me". But now it's fairly obvious—he needs someone who can look past it all, someone seemingly immune to the gorgeous face, the arrogant smile and the celeb status. He needs exactly what he thanked me for being earlier—a friend.

"Fine. I'll see you at noon."

"Wear something you don't mind getting dirty. And what size shoe do you wear?"

"The more I hear about this, the more likely I am to change my mind."

"But you won't. What size?"

"Six."

"Okay. See you tomorrow."

I step outside into the cool Georgia afternoon as Branch pulls up in the driveway. He said I should wear something I don't mind getting dirty, so I'm dressed in distressed jeans and a blue-and-white flannel shirt. Since the weather in Georgia is known to change every two to three hours, layers are the way to go, so I'm wearing a blue T-shirt underneath.

Falling asleep ended up being quite the task last night. I may have gotten in about four hours so I'm sure I look a little worse for wear. I'd sworn against seeing this guy ever again but I can't in good conscious turn away from him when he's hurting over the loss of someone as significant in his life as Jimmy had been. Will I pay for it later? Probably so. But I'll deal with that as it comes.

When Branch hops out of the SUV with a bag in his hand, his lips curve into a smile that stirs the butterflies in my belly. *He's happy to see me.* And that knowledge emits feelings of both awkwardness and elation at the same time.

"Hey, sugar."

"Hey, *sugar*," I mimic. "What's in the bag?"

He grasps my hand and tugs me behind him. "Your boots."

Boots? Why would I need those?

He reaches over into the SUV and presses a button, then the hatch at the rear of the vehicle slowly lifts. We walk around back and he tells me to have a seat. When I do, he goes down on one knee, lifts my right foot, untying my laces and slipping off my shoe. He repeats the same with my other foot, then goes for the box in the bag. He removes the lid, slides a boot onto each socked foot, then laces and ties each. I notice he's wearing boots too and they also look brand new. When he's done, he grasps my hand again and urges me to stand.

"Feel okay?" he asks.

"Yeah but—"

"You'll see," he replies before I can finish my question. "Let's go."

With his hand at my back, he guides me to the passenger side and opens my door. I hop in and buckle up as he rounds the hood to the driver's side.

Although I'm not a fan of the unexpected, I have to admit I'm excited to see what he's planned. A nearly two-hour drive leads us to the small town of Tallulah Falls. Branch announces we're hiking to the water falls for a picnic. It's my first time visiting this part of Georgia and I've heard the falls rival those of Niagara. I don't tell him, but this sounds like the perfect outing.

We follow the signs for the Shortline Trail and endeavor a three-mile hike on the paved line that follows the Old Tallulah Falls Railroad Bed. As we move along the trail, Branch tells me about his visit with Loretta this morning. Her sister had arrived and will be staying on well after the baby is born. He also tells me about the content of the papers he'd reviewed with Loretta. It was a copy of Jimmy's will, and he'd left the garage and the Corvette to Branch.

For years, he'd hounded Jimmy to sell the car, but he never considered any of Branch's offers—even the one that was triple the car's value. After all his attempts to purchase it, Branch never imagined he'd actually own it, especially not this way. And the garage…it holds memories that he could never place a price on. The car and the garage…they both owned a piece of Jimmy's soul.

That explains the look I'd seen in Branch's eyes the evening before. Two things that meant the world to Jimmy now belong to Branch.

When my stomach angrily announces its need for food, he laughs as I follow him to a spot near the falls. He slides the backpack from my shoulders, pulls out a blanket and spreads it over the grass. Then I watch as he assembles lunch from the backpack he was carrying.

"I could help, you know."

"Yeah, but you always serve others so I figure it's okay to give you a break today. Sit," he says gesturing at the spot across from him.

I shrug and do what he says, quickly finding myself deep in conversation about Cecelia and Noah as Branch passes out small details about Jace and his parents. In response to a heart-to-heart the previous night with his dad Curtis, Branch admits that he agreed to extend more of an effort to make peace with his newly reconciled family. Curtis also requested Branch's blessing to ask Mary to renew their vows.

I easily infer that his change of heart is a direct correlation to losing Jimmy. What else would explain his softening view for the man he'd told me just yesterday he resents?

For lunch, we have chicken salad on whole wheat, some green drink that Branch insists is good for me, and an apple. I figured he picked up the chicken salad but was surprised when he explains how he made it fresh this morning.

Later as we stand near the falls, he tells me about his life in Dallas. He even extends an invitation so that I can see his paintings.

"Come here," he says, tugging me closer. "Pine needle." He picks it from my hair, then looks down at me. "If you were any farther away I'd swear we didn't come here together."

I angle my head to the side, studying his face. "I can't get too close, I may get burned," I reply with a smirk. "After all, you are *The Man on Fire*."

"That's on the field. So don't feed me that bullshit."

"I'm not so sure it only applies there."

"Why is that?"

"I recall reading somewhere about a trail of broken hearts."

He chuckles. "Again, I call bullshit."

"Maybe you should have your press agent get on that."

We both laugh, our gazes fixed on each other.

"Yeah, I'll give Connie a call so she can straighten all of that out. Just so *you* know, I haven't had a relationship with a woman since I left Blue Ridge."

My brows rise. "Oh, so you're into *men* now? No big deal if you have a boyfriend, you know…since I'm into three-somes and all."

We share another laugh, thinking back to the day in the diner when he introduced the topic of him hooking up with me and my *girlfriend.*

"Sorry about that," he says, a grin still on his lips. "Ragan."

"See, you can call me by my name, I always knew you could, *sugar.*"

He cocks his head and lifts a brow. His blue eyes are both impassioned and mischievous as they travel my face. I combat the blush that creeps to my cheeks. And I ignore the flip-flop of my stomach as his gaze pins me to this spot. Those tactics last but mere seconds before I'm falling into the abyss of his wonderment. I swallow as he studies me like he's discovering something for the first time.

"May I kiss you?" he asks.

"You're asking…you want to…huh?"

"I didn't think I was speaking a foreign language." He leans closer, his lips a hairsbreadth away from mine. "Ragan Prescott, I'm asking for your permission to kiss you. Are you going to deny me that?"

"N—" he cuts off my words, his lips already moving slowly over mine. He kisses me for what feels like forever, his tongue sweeping against mine, his hands at my nape, holding me in place. A tiny moan vibrates up my throat and I gently tug at his shirt to bring him closer. And for several moments in time, that's where we stand—immersed in a kiss that I know I'll never forget. No sooner does that thought enter my head does Branch murmur at my mouth, then pull away.

His eyes are alive with the excitement I'm certain he sees in mine. "Thank you."

"Er…you're welcome." Why is he thanking me? And what just happened? I quickly tell myself this all must be a reaction to losing Jimmy so I figure I'll just go with it. Yeah, I'll just go with it.

Truth be told, if he wanted to kiss me a thousand times, I'd let him. And I won't dare admit this to anyone but no use in lying to myself—I'm not here just because he needs me. Quite frankly, I think I'd do most anything to spend time with him. I know it's a horrible idea. And I also know nothing good can come from falling for a man like Branch, but it's too late.

#Fallen

Chapter
TWENTY-ONE

Branch

EVERYTHING ABOUT RAGAN SPEAKS TO A PAST THAT demands she build walls around her heart. But the softness in her brown eyes tells me she'll lower them just enough to let me in. She'll go against her better judgment and take a chance on me. And I'll do to her just what I did in the past. It's best if she decides she wants nothing to do with me. But I know I'm not selfless enough to let that happen.

My gaze caresses her face, falling to the curve of her lips. *My cock would look so fucking hot between those lips.* I notice her accelerated breathing and when I look into her eyes they tell me she knows exactly what I'm thinking. *Something that I shouldn't. Not with her. Not again.* Swallowing, I grasp her hands and bring her palms to my lips with a gentle kiss. Her fingers are cold. And trembling. She's afraid. And she has every right to be. That acknowledgement serves as my wake-up call. I need to let this go.

"How about we grab some coffee before we head back?" I ask.

"Er...sure." Confusion flutters across her face, then a slight smile tugs at the corner of her mouth. "Sounds good."

"And if you're up to it, we can check out some of the local artwork."

The brown of her eyes lights to a honey-gold. "Yes, I'd like that."

"Cool. Let's pack up." I step around her, refusing to succumb to a temptation that shouldn't be there in the first place.

After the lunch supplies are stowed in the backpacks, we sling them over our shoulders, then retrace our steps along the trail. Ragan goes on and on about Noah and how great it is to reach out to him whenever she wants. I ask about the relationship between her dad and brother. She says David isn't aware of their reconnection, and Noah demands they keep it that way. I can't say I blame him. I actually don't understand how she can live under the same roof with him.

After two cups of coffee and a half hour in one of the art galleries, we're on the road headed back to Blue Ridge. I ask Ragan more about her own drawings, and this time she appears more at ease sharing her passion for art. She explains how it haphazardly began as a way to express the pain she was unable to articulate. She goes on further to say her finished works chronicle a journey of growth and self-discovery. Although her inspiration stems from a place of sadness—other than when she speaks of Noah and Cecelia—this is the only time I've heard pure happiness in her voice.

The wintry Georgia afternoon has bled into evening when we finally arrive at her dad's house. I turn off the ignition and exhale a sigh. "As far as surprises go, that wasn't a bad one, right?"

"No. It wasn't *entirely* horrible."

"What?" I ask when I see she wants to say more.

"But it was kinda confusing. Can I ask you something?"

My thoughts skip back to the morning after we'd had sex when she voiced the same question—to say I was less than amicable back then is an understatement. "Go ahead."

"The night we had um…that we—"

"Hooked up?"

"Yeah," she replies and averts her eyes. "You regret it happened and you want to forget about it. Right?"

"Not exactly," I reply, wondering if I should tell her more, ultimately deciding that I will. "Thing is…I can't forget about it." I recline my head on the back of the seat and look over at Ragan. "That's why I was with Skye the day after. I was trying to get you out of my head and I figured the best way to do that was to do what I've always done."

"But it was only a few hours after you and I—." She shakes her head as if she doesn't want to revisit that scene.

"Yeah, a few hours that fucked my head up. Full disclosure?"

She shrugs. "Why not?"

"I don't think about women that I've fucked, Ragan. Ever. So it threw me for a loop when I realized it was different with you…that you weren't slipping out of my head as easily as the others. The only time a woman intrudes my thoughts is right before I fuck her. When I'm done with her, I'm done."

The disappointment of my confession washes over her face.

"That's kind of cold, don't you think?"

"It's who I am. I have a very healthy sexual appetite, always have. But that's all I have an appetite for when it comes to women. And I'm glad it's that way."

"Then what am I doing here?"

That's a question I have yet to figure out. I care about her but I have no idea why. The dare to have sex with her, the piss-poor decision to hook up with Skye the day after, then the fight which led to the decision to steer clear of each other…yeah, I'd really fucked things up with her, yet here she is giving me another chance to do what? Fuck with her head again?

"You're a friend," I say, hoping those words sate her curiosity.

"And you always kiss your friends?"

This conversation is over. I've already said and done too much with her. "Let me grab your shoes and walk you to the door." I hop out of the SUV and wait for her to catch up.

"I'll admit, today *was* fun," she says when we're a few feet from the house.

"Yeah, thanks for going with me."

"No problem." She looks at me with those same questions in her eyes.

"What is it, Ragan?"

"So you've never fallen in love with or even considered a relationship with anyone you've slept with?"

I grin at her persistence. She wants answers I don't have and others I know she won't like. I don't want a relationship or anything close to it, so whatever I have with her shouldn't mean shit to me…but it does, so I try to skate around her question. "Are you asking for yourself? Are you falling for me?"

She blushes and turns away. "Uh…nope."

I touch a finger under her chin and draw her eyes back to mine. "That was a quick answer."

"When you're sure, it should come quick."

She falls quiet again, studying me. "But what if I were? What if I, Ragan Prescott, were falling for *The Man on Fire*?"

"So you'd what? Want me to be your *person*?"

"Hypothetically."

I shake my head. "Hypothetical or not, I wouldn't wish that on any woman. I don't look at women that way."

"Exactly how do you look at women?"

"Let's just say I'm not a good man. At least not the kind of good you need. You've seen that for yourself." I tuck a stray hair behind her ear, lean over and drop a kiss to her forehead—a gesture that seemed involuntary and one that I regret as soon as I look into her eyes. "As for love, that part of me doesn't work. You deserve better. You need someone who's gonna treat you the way you deserve to be treated, not someone who's gonna practice on you and then throw you away like I would. You've been through enough."

"But I didn't say it was me."

"You didn't have to."

"Whatever. You're just a big old mass of confusion…as usual."

Chapter
TWENTY-TWO

Branch

SOMEHOW I MAKE IT THROUGH THE FUNERAL. AND now that I'm at Loretta and Jimmy's, the devastation of the loss slams into me all over again. Jimmy's gone. He won't be walking through the front door with flowers for his wife or surprise gifts for his daughters. He won't sit and watch games with me or fly out to see me play. There will be no more bullshitting or life lessons at the garage. No more wisdom from a man I respected more than anyone.

I lift my gaze from the Perez family photo I've been focused on for the better part of an hour and spot Ragan. She's been keeping Jimmy's girls entertained, helping with the food, and consoling a woman she barely knows. I can see why she made such an impression on Jimmy. She's truly a good person. And once you get past the attitude, you see it. A kindheartedness. So altruistic and genuine, it's as involuntary as the beat of her heart. She's a rare one. That's for sure. Someone who's been beaten down by life and given every reason to be negative usually is, but not her. She's an amazing woman, but she's learned to protect herself. And after hearing her story, I get it. She was given a bum deal even before she was born into this world. My mother had been a mess on most days, but at least I had her. And despite the guilt trips, the arguments, and the shit with Dad, I knew she loved me. How does a *girl* go through life never knowing that? That her mother loves her? Wants her? If guys—even assholes like me—need that, certainly women need it more. But Ragan, she's had to grow up without it. She's never had it and she never will.

She looks up from Loretta and takes in the expressions of those around her, her perusal stopping with me. The meek smile she's been wearing all day falls when she realizes I'm watching her. She knows this has cut me deep—that I'm suffering right along with Jimmy's family. When she starts toward me, I shake my head, signaling that I don't need the comfort she's been giving to virtual strangers all day. I turn the other way and head outside for some air.

I'm in my head, trying to sort through the next steps I'll have to take. Steps I'd never make if Jimmy were still here. But his death leaves me little-to-no choice.

A while later, Ragan is beside me. She takes my hand and threads her fingers through mine, and I don't resist. I take comfort in her touch. She doesn't say anything. She's just here. And she's exactly what I need and don't need at the same time.

Jimmy will be missed. And he'll be remembered as more than just the guy who fixed cars or sat on the city council. He'll be remembered as a family man, as a great father, and as a wonderful husband. Earlier, I listened as Loretta shared kind words and stories about her life with Jimmy. She spoke of his family traditions. Of the memories that define the context of their lives.

And now I wonder about myself.

What will happen after *I'm* gone?

What will I be remembered for? That I hooked up with women that I didn't give a fuck about? That I didn't have anyone to carry on family traditions? What will be said at my funeral? That I was a great football player? That I had a *gift*? Sure, there will be the football legacy. But there won't be a *true* legacy of Branch McGuire. Is that what Jimmy was trying to tell me?

Knowing I have to be in Dallas for a while to meet with my agents, the team, and the coaches, I spend every spare minute with Loretta and the girls, often including Mama, Jace, and Dad. Loretta is doing her best to keep up appearances in front of her daughters, but I see how much it's taking out of her. To pretend she's okay when in actuality she's anything but.

She's been ordered to remain on bedrest until the baby is born. And after spending time with Loretta, I think a part of her is glad to have a valid reason to step away from everyone. She gets to be alone and give in to the grief she tries to hide from well-wishers. But I see it in her eyes—the sadness, the emptiness, the absolute loss of a man who completed her life.

Time with Jace seems different now. I always enjoy hanging with my kid brother, recognizing parts of myself in him, seeing the admiration in his eyes when he looks up at me—glimpsing the happiness and innocence that still claims him. But over the past week, it's just different. I start to feel more like him. That I want all three—my friends, my parents, and my brother.

Somehow these last few days with my family are the best they've ever been. There are no arguments about Dad, no feelings of guilt about Jace and no manipulation or mental episodes from Mama. For the first time since moving from Blue Ridge years and years ago, I'm not ready to leave.

I even carve out time for Ragan and Cecelia. She's a great little girl. And Ragan is an incredible mother, despite the circumstances that would have made a lesser person fall prey to the demons that I know still haunt her. Ragan pushes past those, determined to be the mom she never had...that she will never have.

I'm still reconciling the pieces of someone else's life that are now my responsibility. Still can't fathom that his garage is now mine. At least temporarily. I plan to sign it over to his kids when they are of age. It should go to them—not me. As for the Corvette, I'm not sure what to do with it. Drive it? Memorialize it? Either way, it's another piece of Jimmy I never expected.

Chapter
TWENTY-THREE

Ragan

SLIDING OUT OF THE CAR, I LET OUT A SIGH, FLICK THE key fob and head toward the house. Behind me, I hear what sounds like footsteps rapidly slapping against the pavement. Distracted by my ringtone, I grab my phone, spin around, then *wham!* The breath is knocked from my lungs and my body is flung to the ground. Someone is on top of me, and the rancid odor of fish floods my sinuses. That's when I know the damp hand covering my mouth belongs to Ethan.

"*Arrested?* You had me fucking arrested? Did you think that would end us?"

I shake my head back and forth, then yank his hand away. "I didn't have you arrested. Your crazy behavior took care of that. Now get off." I shove his chest and writhe under the weight of his frame.

"You're coming back home with me and everything's going back to the way it was. Do you understand?"

"That's never going to fucking happen. In fact, if you were the last guy on the planet, I'd never be with you."

"I don't know what you're trying to prove, Ragan. Are you trying to hurt me?"

"If I wanted to hurt you, that would mean I care, which I don't."

"Why?" He leans in, his lips inches from mine. "Because you're giving it up to that ball player?"

"That's none of your business."

"You're mine. Everything you do is my business."

"I'm warning you. Get off."

"*You're* warning me?"

"I promise I'll scream my head off and you'll land right back in jail, you fucking psycho."

A large hand curls around my throat as the other comes down hard across my cheek. "You belong to me. Every part of you is mine."

"Stop it. You're fucking crazy." I grasp a handful of his hair and try to yank it from his fucking scalp. "You and I are done. When are you going to get that through your head?"

"That's where you're wrong, bitch. We will *never* be over. You got that? Never!"

My body thrashes beneath his and he loses his grip. I manage to pull another arm from underneath him and land a fierce strike to his nose, drawing blood. I roll to the side, snake free, then scream for help.

I continue my retreat, crawling a few feet, then scrambling to stand upright, but he trips me and I'm back on the ground, falling face-first into a pile of mud.

"Do you think I'm going to sit by while you fuck another man? Do you? Huh?" Ethan grasps my ankles and flips me over, then I'm met with a fierce kick to my side.

"No! Please. Stop!" I yell, but the blunt edge of his boot meets my ribcage again and I feel the bones breaking inside me. "Help. Someone help me!" I cry out as Ethan falls to the ground and straddles my frame.

When he sees a drop of his blood land on my cheek, he loses another shred of his sanity, striking the side of my head with a solid punch that takes my vision. But it doesn't stop there. He strikes me again…and again. I try to block the evil torrent of blows, but his fists come hard and steady.

"Where is your protector now? Huh? Where is he?"

"Eth… St…" I try to spit out the words but the excruciating pain takes over every nerve ending in my body. A single pulse beats inside me and then everything shuts down. The light is gone and silence swallows me whole. I hear nothing…not even the sound of my cries.

My eyes barely open, allowing only a trace of light to pass through. I reach for my face and feel gauze, then I move my hands over my torso and it's as if I'm not moving at all. My entire body is numb—I feel nothing. My lips part to speak and I swear I say "what's going on?", but I don't hear the words. I've no voice. Panic overtakes me and my chest rises and falls abnormally fast. Something isn't right. *What's wrong with me?*

"She's waking up," I hear someone say. I'm not sure who it is, but it's a man's voice.

I can't smell anything either. *Why can't I smell?*

"Call the doctor. Let him know she's finally coming out of the coma. I can't believe it's been a whole week," comes another voice. This time it's a woman. Was that Aunt Sophie? And why would she be calling a doctor? For who? *What the hell is going on?*

I struggle to find my words again. I swallow, and this time when I speak, I actually hear myself, but it comes out as undecipherable drivel.

I try to move but it's as if a cement block is holding me down. After three failed attempts, I give up and lie there, trapped inside my body. I hear more voices but this time I can't make out what's being said. I try again to claw my way to the surface and make heads or tails of what's happened to me. But something in my head is pushing me back under. Refusing to give up, I utter another string of unintelligible gibberish, then I'm pushed further into the darkness of which I'm trying to escape. I can see it—a black cavernous hole with tentacles and it's reaching for me.

"I…I…please."

It grabs me.

Wrapping itself around my frame until I'm no more.

Then I'm out again.

"Please. Don't. Please. I'll be good. I promise."

The response is a slap across my back.

"You don't know what good is," she shouts.

Another bite into my skin.

A deep, visceral cry escapes. It's a cry for help. A cry that will go unanswered.

The lashes across my back are quick and deep. I know she's drawing blood this time. I just know it. I shake my head, turning it to the side, and gasp for air. "Cassidy, please, please stop!"

My eyes shoot open, wet with tears, as pain radiates through what feels like most of my body.

It was a dream. It was just a dream. But it wasn't. It was a memory of the day Cassidy caught me slipping from my room for something to eat after being sent to bed without dinner. It was a recollection of the day she beat me with such fierce brutality that I missed school for three days.

Where the hell am I?

After taking some time to process my surroundings, I realize it's a new day. And like the previous one, I'm not alone.

"Sounds like you had a nightmare," he says, stepping closer to the bed. "Are you okay? Can I get you anything?"

It takes everything in me to turn toward the sound of the voice. When I finally do, my eyes fall upon the beauty and perfection of an angel. I'm obviously still dreaming because *he* wouldn't be here. Not with me…not like this.

I touch my face, the gauze is gone.

I try to push myself up, but I can't seem to move. He stares at me, smooths a hand over my hair, then leans in and kisses my forehead. When his woodsy scent hits my nose, I accept that he isn't a figment of my imagination. He's actually here.

"Try to keep still," he says.

I'm in too much pain to be embarrassed, but the look in his eyes says I should be. Then I remember where I am and who put me here. "How did you know I was in the hospital?" My voice sounds strange. As if my vocal cords are stuffed with wads of cotton.

"You weren't at work."

I try to clear my throat. "So you figured I was in the hospital? That's quite a leap."

He places a straw in a cup of water and brings it to my lips. I look up at him as I take a sip. "Actually, Carrie told me."

I let out a groan. "Figures."

"It wasn't like that. Don't be angry with her."

"This was not her business to tell."

He shakes his head. "Alert for only a couple of minutes and grouchy already."

"This is personal," I croak, my words coming slowly. "Not anything for her to go gabbing about."

"Since you and I are on good terms, I'd started dropping by the diner again."

"Yeah. So?"

"I asked her a couple of times where you were and she said you were off. It was obvious something was up, so on the third day, I demanded she tell me what was going on. She still hesitated but when I offered her an autographed jersey, she finally caved."

"Like I said…figures."

He strokes a finger over my cheek. "I was worried about you."

"Why?"

"Well, turns out I had reason to be. I'm gonna kick that fucker's ass."

"Leave it alone, Branch," I reply, the strain in my voice gradually fading. "I think he's lost his mind and the more I defend myself, the crazier he'll become. And I have my daughter to think about."

"Did he do this because of me?"

"He's upset because I won't come back to him. And because I pressed charges. And because he's embarrassed."

His brows furrow. "What the fuck does he have to be embarrassed about?"

"He was arrested at his job. In front of his boss and his friends. And yes, he did mention you."

The door swings open and a nurse walks in with a tray of food. "Glad to see you're finally awake, Ragan. I'm Nurse Debra. How are you feeling?"

"Like I've been thrown under a bus, run over twice, then used for a speed bump." I grimace a smile.

"You'll be good as new in no time. The doctor says you're healing quite well."

"That's good to hear." Although it sure doesn't feel like it.

"I took a chance you'd be awake and grabbed some food for you. Can you manage to feed yourself or do you think you'll need help?"

I want to say I'll manage on my own but I can barely hold my head up.

"I'll do it," Branch suggests.

I frown at his offer. "Er...no, you won't."

Nurse Debra gives Branch a lingering once-over and then looks back to me with a raised brow. "I thought the meds had worn off by now."

"Jeez. Not you, too. Why is everyone so easily sucked in by this guy?"

Branch chuckles. "Obviously not everyone."

Debra places the tray on the table then looks up at me. "So what's it gonna be, Miss Ragan?"

"He can do it, I guess."

She gives me a wink. "Lucky girl. I'll be back with your meds after you've eaten," she adds, and heads out of the room.

"Do you know how many women would die to have me at their bedside? Let alone feed them?"

I roll my eyes. "Oh, let me guess…hundreds."

"Try millions."

I laugh. "Ow."

"Are you okay?" he asks, his gaze soft on mine. "Do you need me to call the nurse back?"

"No, I'm fine. Stop making me laugh."

Branch removes the lid from the tray of food and frowns. "Tomorrow I'll bring you something in. This looks like shit."

"Tomorrow? You mean you're coming back?"

"Hey, don't pretend as if you don't like the thought of seeing my pretty face again tomorrow. Now open up." He holds a spoon of soup in front of me.

I exhale a sigh and part my lips.

"Wider," he orders.

"I hate this." I follow his instruction, then he slides the spoon of noodles into my mouth.

"That's a good girl," he says, grinning back at me.

"Oh, fuck off."

"Hey, is that the thanks I get?"

"I'm sorry," I say after a second spoonful. "Sometimes, it's kind of hard to be nice to you."

"Even after…"

"Yeah, especially after that. The way it ended was really messed up. Just like the first time we had sex."

Some of the soup dribbles from the spoon as his eyes dart

to mine. "What?"

"Nothing."

"No. Tell me. What are you talking about?"

"I promised myself I wouldn't say anything but…the night of the bonfire wasn't the only time we'd had sex. The first time was in high school."

"If this is your idea of a joke, I think you're confused on how to deliver a punch line."

"I'm not joking. And before you ask, it's not the drugs talking. You and I really did have sex."

He looks at me as if he's trying to determine if I really am setting him up for a joke. "And where was I, because I think I'd remember something like that."

"Not really."

"Okay, why do you say that?"

"Because you're Branch McGuire."

His brows scrunch. "What does that have to do with anything?"

"I guess I need to jar your memory. It was the night of the homecoming game between Dawson and Blue Ridge. Zaxby's—the restaurant I worked for—was catering the homecoming after-party. I was working that night, otherwise I would've never been allowed out of the house. Anyway, you were beyond wasted and I kinda had a mega crush on you back then, so you were conveniently in my line of vision for a large part of the night."

He offers a few more spoons of soup between details of my story.

"You were goofing around with your boys—as usual—and you grabbed a bottle of water from one of the tubs, then you turned around and bumped right smack into me.

I went sprawling on my ass. You reached down to help me but I pulled you down with me and I kissed you. Surprisingly enough, we didn't stop. We ended up behind the stadium and that's where it happened. As soon as we finished, we headed back to the party and one of the cheerleaders came up to you and pulled you away. You looked back at me for a split second…and that was it."

Branch holds the spoon in midair. "Are you remembering correctly?"

"It was the night I lost my virginity. I don't think a girl would forget something like that."

Horrified by my admission, the spoon falls from his hand. "So you're saying I took your virginity?"

"Not so much as *took,* as it is that I gave it to you."

"Are you sure? That it was me, I mean?"

I roll my eyes. "Do you seriously think a girl would ever forget her first time?"

He falls quiet, his eyes searching mine for answers. "Your first time? And it was with *me*? Why would you do something like that? And outside? Why me?"

"Why *not* you? You were Branch McGuire, the most sought-after guy in two counties and I was a high school girl with a silly crush." I shrug. "You gave someone like me a second look. Granted it was a drunken look, but no way was I going to let that pass me by."

He's quiet again.

"What's wrong?" I ask.

A look of remorse clouds his expression. "I'm sorry for not remembering."

My gaze falls to the tray of food. "Whatever."

"I'm serious."

"A guy like you doesn't remember stuff like that, so I'm not surprised."

"Is that why you were so…opposed to me when I started coming to the diner?"

"That's just one of the many reasons," I reply.

Branch finishes feeding me but he doesn't say much more. Not even his egotistical jokes. Once he's sure I'm comfortable, he leaves me alone, but not before grabbing my phone and adding his number. I stare after him as he walks out, wondering how in God's name I've become friends with Branch McGuire.

Chapter
TWENTY-FOUR

Branch

"**M**AMA'S IN LABOR!" LUCIANA'S VOICE COMES loud and winded through the phone.

I toss the wrench aside and wipe my hands on my jeans. "Are your aunts there?"

"No, they're out picking up some last minute stuff for the nursery."

"Have you called an ambulance?" I ask.

"Mama wanted us to call you first."

"Okay. Jimmy had mentioned something about a go-bag."

"Yeah, Isidora's grabbing it now."

"I'm on my way," I say and rush out of the garage.

"It's a boy," Loretta says looking up at me with big tears in her eyes.

A son. *Jimmy has a son.* "Man. Jimmy would have been screaming it down the halls."

Loretta wipes the water from her eyes. "I think he's screaming it up in heaven."

The kids all circle around Loretta as she looks down at the latest addition to their family.

"You okay, Mama?" Isidora asks.

"*Sí, bebé.* I'm just happy…and a little sad that your dad isn't here to help with the three-in-the-morning feedings."

"What are we going to name him?" Tater asks.

She looks at me, then down at the baby. "Jimmy Warren Perez."

My middle name. I don't know what shocks me more, the fact that Loretta knows it or that her newborn is now my namesake. I stare at the two of them, too dumbfounded to do much more than manage a grin that I'm sure looks as awkward as I feel right now.

Tater sits on the bed to get a closer look at the baby. "I like that, Mama."

"Me too," the girls chime in.

"Your father wouldn't have let me name his boy anything other than Jimmy. And he's always thought of you as a son," she adds, peering up at me. "So it's the perfect name."

I nod at her choice. "I actually think Jimmy would approve."

"I know he would," she says. "Would you like to hold him?"

I shake my head and take a step back. "I don't think that's a good idea. Maybe when he's a little bigger."

"Oh, come on. He won't break."

I'm about to refuse again but something urges me to

reconsider. "Er…sure."

When Little Jimmy's nestled in my arms, I look down at him and smile. "He's…uh."

"I know he's a bit funny looking right now," Loretta says. "It's okay, you can say it."

"Well, I was trying to see which of you he resembled, but at the moment, he looks more like a different species."

Loretta and the girls share a laugh. My gaze scans the merriment of their expressions. I'm glad I can give them something to smile about in spite of the emotional turmoil their lives have become over the last few weeks.

Little Jimmy makes a delicate noise and my eyes fall back to the tiny one in my arms. I see a new life—a small defenseless being dependent on us to get everything just right. I skip ahead to the next several years and I see Jace and the need for his stability. And finally, I see Cecelia—an innocent little girl who's never had either of those things. An unfamiliar feeling settles over me, then I look up and see Loretta and the girls watching my interaction with the baby. I really want to be the stand-up guy they'll need. I want to be the type of man and mentor to them that Jimmy was to me.

"I'll bet he'll be the spitting image of his dad," Loretta says, when I eventually pass him back to her. "God wouldn't have it any other way." She looks at the baby and then at each of her daughters. "He's given me the most precious parts of my Jimmy."

Chapter
TWENTY-FIVE

Ragan

AFTER A TWO WEEK STINT AT FANNIN REGIONAL Hospital, I finally get my walking papers. My face still looks as if it was used as a punching bag. And I suppose it kinda was. The two broken ribs are healing nicely according to the X-rays, but it's still a bitch to sit or stand. I'll be out of work for the next three to four weeks at least.

My ex is in jail where he belongs…with quite a hefty bail. I have a feeling Branch had something to do with that. No way can the Tylers come up with enough money to get Ethan out any time soon. And with that worry off my mind, I can focus on getting better and taking care of CeeCee.

I slide my feet into the pink fuzzy slippers Branch bought me the week before, then pull my new jacket—another gift from Branch—from the closet.

A knock sounds at the door as I step toward the bed. "Come in."

"Are you about ready to go?" Branch asks.

My heart flip-flops each time I look at him, so of course I'm happy he's here but he's not who I expected to walk through the door. "I thought Dad and Aunt Sophie were coming for me."

"They were."

I stuff the last of my toiletries in the bag. "So why are you here?"

He shrugs. "I offered to do it."

"And why did you do that?"

"Ragan, as strange as it is, we're friends now. And friends help friends. How often must I repeat that before it sinks in?"

I stare at him, unsure how to reply.

"You do know what a friend is right?" he asks, his voice dripping with sarcasm.

Before Ethan? *Yes.* During and after Ethan? *No.* It's almost as if I'm learning to walk amongst the living again. How could I have not seen what he was doing to me? Or maybe I'd seen it all along, but I was just in too deep to fight my way out.

The orderly comes in with a wheelchair before I can answer. "If you're ready, I'll give you a ride downstairs."

"I've got it," Branch tells him.

"I kinda have to do it," the orderly replies. "Hospital policy."

"Well, in this case, I'll be the one to do it. Branch McGuire policy."

The dark-haired boy appears at a loss for words as Branch reaches for the chair.

I wince as I go to put on my jacket and Branch rushes over to help me. He then grabs my bag and slings it across his back.

"I guess I'm ready."

"Your chariot awaits," Branch says, tipping his head toward the chair.

I shake my head and slowly lower myself into the seat, then Branch wheels me out of the room, down the hall and to the elevators. We eventually roll through the front doors of the hospital. And at the foot of the walkway is a truck I don't recognize. Once we're settled inside, I ask, "Is this Jimmy's?"

"Mine."

"I've never seen you in this before. Why haven't you ever driven it?"

"It's new."

"You bought it? Why? Aren't you leaving soon?"

"Plans changed."

I look at him, confused by his response and about to ask for more details but he looks away. Does this mean he's staying in Blue Ridge a while longer? The thought alone emits a feeling of happiness I force myself to suppress.

Hmm. If he *is* staying...why? The garage? Nah, that wouldn't keep him here. So maybe it's his family. Maybe he's finally taken Jimmy's advice and is placing the past where it belongs. Maybe he's ready to learn from it instead of trying to outrun it. That's my guess anyways. He doesn't seem open to talking about it, so I don't ask. I look in the opposite direction and stare out the window as we head down Hospital Road.

"Loretta had the baby," he says.

"Really?" I ask, suddenly excited. "How are they?"

"They're fine."

"So..."

He looks over at me, his brow arched.

"Was it a boy?"

"Yep. As a matter of fact it was."

"That's great. I'm so happy for her." At least someone has grasped a fraction of joy in the midst of the hysteria of fucked up-ness. So much has happened in the last few weeks that my head is *still* spinning—sex with Branch, catching him with Skye, the fight with Ethan, Ethan taking CeeCee, Jimmy's death, Ethan kicking my ass, a week in ICU, another week because I wasn't healing as expected, and Branch rescuing me—not once—but twice.

He's visited me at the hospital every day—bringing clothes, fuzzy slippers, a Kindle full of art books, a couple of framed pictures of CeeCee and him at the park with Loretta's girls, and some of the best food I've ever eaten. His mama made most of it but he pitched in with a few of the meals. He even spent the night at the hospital when I was having especially hard days. If I still believed in knights in shining armor, I'd swear Branch polished his just for me. How can he not see that he's the exact opposite of the bad guy he's made himself out to be? Because he's proven it to me over and over.

When I notice we aren't going to Dad's I turn toward him. "Where are you taking me?"

"It's a surprise."

My frame becomes rigid. "I don't like surprises. You know that."

"Too bad."

"I'm serious, Branch. I don't like them. I never have. So take me home. I need to see my daughter."

He half smiles, one corner of his mouth lifting. "Humor me, okay?"

Humor him? What the hell? I want to go home. Irritated

by his ploy, I shake my head and try to figure out what he's up to. Twenty minutes or so later, we turn into one of the nicer subdivisions a few miles outside the edge of town.

"Whose place is this?" I ask, when he pulls to a stop in a driveway.

He shifts the gear to park and presses the button that turns off the ignition. "What if I say it's yours?"

I look over at him, confused. "What are you talking about?"

"Well, actually it *is* yours. I closed on it a couple of days ago."

My mouth drops open. "You did what?"

"It's a gift."

"*Gift?* Normal folks don't just go around buying houses as gifts."

His self-assured smile disappears and his expression turns serious. "There's nothing normal about any of this, Ragan. You've been through a lot. More than any person should in one lifetime. More than anyone should *ever*. You need a break. And I'm giving it to you."

"I'm not some type of project or charity case."

"I didn't say you were."

"Please take me to my Dad's."

"Why?"

"Because that's where I live."

"But you don't have to and I know you don't want to. Remember the day on the steps at my place? You told me about your mom, your dad, your stepmom, and the house you grew up in, and how difficult it was for you to be there."

"Yeah, so?"

"You don't have to be there anymore."

"I don't like where I live, so you just go out and buy me a house? That's crazy."

"What's crazy is that you're staying somewhere that's holding you hostage to a past you want no part of."

"That's my problem. And I'll figure it out."

"What about Cecelia?"

"What about her?" I ask.

"You said you didn't want her there. And I don't want her there either. It's not good for either of you."

I fall quiet and reluctantly glance back at the house. It's a really nice place. I mean *really* nice. And the lawn is immaculate—just like I always imagined for my own home one day. There's even a tire swing hanging from the large Oak tree in the front yard.

"Just come inside and take a look and if you absolutely hate it, I'll call the realtor and tell her to put it back on the market."

Branch gets out of the truck and gestures for me to follow suit but my stubbornness won't allow me to move. He lets out a sigh and strides to the passenger side and opens the door. "Stop being ridiculous and get out."

I cross my arms over my chest and look in the opposite direction. Moments later, his hands are sliding beneath my thighs lifting me from the seat.

"Goddamnit, Ragan."

He carries me with more ease than I would have expected. But then again, the jeans that barely sit at my waist indicate I *have* dropped even more pounds.

"I don't know why you have to make everything so fucking difficult," he grumbles.

"And I don't get why you're doing this. Put me down."

"I just told you why."

"But it can't be *just* that."

"Why? Because you don't deserve some good luck every once in a while?"

He places me on my feet when we're near the front door. I look up at him for more of an answer, his blue eyes gleaming back at me.

"And maybe it's a little more than just that," he says and pulls a key from his pocket. "I took something from you a long time ago. So this is my way of giving something back."

My brows scrunch. "Is this because of what happened between us in high school?"

"Yeah. But mostly because I don't think you enjoy going home to a place that's full of bad shit. And I don't want that for you," he says, looking down at me, his gaze tender. "If you want to start a new life, you have to wake up in a new life, not in the same one that gave you nightmares."

That much is true. I hate that fucking place but I can't accept this. "I don't accept handouts."

"Good, because I don't give 'em." His hand is at the small of my back, urging me inside. "I expect you to pay rent on time every month."

If I thought the outside of the house was nice, I'm positively stunned now that I take in the interior. "You know I can't afford this, right?"

"Take a look at your expenses and let me know what fits your budget and that's what you'll pay me."

"You can't be serious."

"I said it. Didn't I?"

"I don't know," I say, scanning the space a second time. "This just doesn't feel right."

"If it makes you feel better, we'll draw up a rental agreement. That way it's a run-of-the-mill business transaction."

I step further into the house and look around. It's completely furnished, and I have to admit I love everything I've seen so far. There's nothing "run-of-the-mill" about any of this.

"There is one catch."

I slowly turn to face him. "I knew it. What?"

"No more of the attitude when I come to Jim Bob's for lunch."

"Seriously?"

"Yup."

"That's your stipulation?" I ask.

"Too challenging for you?"

"No, I can be nice to people. Especially if they're nice to me. Which you never were in the beginning, but I suppose I can lose the attitude. I mean, I kinda have to now. Can't have my landlord on the outs with me."

He flashes a grin. "So you'll accept it? You'll live here?"

"Yes. I'd have to be crazy to refuse this. But I have a question."

"Sure. What is it?"

"I really don't get why you just don't eat someplace else. Why keep coming to Jim Bob's? The food ain't that great."

His gaze skates over my face, settling on my eyes. "Maybe I keep coming for you."

Huh. The doorbell rings before I can figure out if he means what I *think* he means.

"That's probably your folks bringing Cecelia by. I'll get out of your hair and let you get settled."

"You're leaving?" I ask, surprised by the disappointment

in my tone.

"Yeah, but I'll see you at the diner soon. And remember. Lose the attitude."

A few days later, I'm standing in the bathroom looking in the mirror. Half my face is swollen from the stitches in my cheek. Most of the other bruises are gone. The ones that aren't can be covered with makeup. I'm a pro at that—been covering bruises since I was seven years old.

With CeeCee having gone to church with Aunt Sophie, I wander around the house, still in awe that I live here. That it's mine. Well, sort of anyway. Everything is so nice. Nothing I'd be able to repay Branch for anytime soon.

I flip on the TV as my phone sounds notifying me of a text.

Branch: Do you still not like surprises? Because I have one more.
Ragan: What have you done now?
Branch: I'll tell you in a couple of days. I need to give you time to stop being pissy about the first one.

I stare at his message and smile. Me? Ragan Prescott. Friends with Branch McGuire. It still doesn't quite register. And I never did reach a conclusion on what he meant by coming to the diner for me? No way was that anything more than another one of his weird innuendos. Maybe, just maybe

I can come to accept a friendship with the sexy-as-sin foot-ball star I'd secretly obsessed over in high school, but no way could it ever be more than that. Like vodka and decisions, we're simply a bad mix. I'm the single mother trying to get her life on track and he's the record-breaking NFL player try-ing to parlay his success.

Chapter
TWENTY-SIX

Branch

RAGAN PRESCOTT.

She continues to surprise me.

There she was…being released from the hospital, her arm in a sling and her face battered and bruised, yet she was still smiling at the good fortune of someone else. She was genuinely happy for Loretta. I saw it in her eyes. I saw it in her smile, and I heard it in her voice.

No fucking way does she deserve the rotten hand she's been dealt. It pisses me off—even more than I already am—to know that Ethan fucker is still breathing.

I call Connie and tell her to set up a meeting with my attorney. Ethan may have had the upper hand in the past, but I'll be damned if that ever happens again. He's seen his last days of hoarding any kind of power over Ragan. Of that I'll make sure.

I disconnect the call, draft the email and hit Send, already knowing Andrés is going to lose his shit when he sees the images. Before I can even return the phone to my pocket, it's ringing.

"That was quick as fuck."

"I want to meet her," he says in a rush.

I pause, unsure as to how that will go over.

"Is that going to be a problem?" he asks.

"No. But I didn't expect you'd move so fast."

"And I didn't expect you to have an eye for this kind of talent. She's a natural."

"I don't know anything about spotting artistic talent. I just know what I like. And some of it resembles what you picked out for Mama."

"She's definitely a talent I've not seen," Andrés says, the excitement in his voice ringing through the phone. "And based on those few drawings alone, I can tell you right now, her work will appeal to a diverse range of art connoisseurs. She's capable of generating sales in a variety of venues. And I want her before someone else scoops her up."

"Want her...as in buying a few of her pieces?"

"No, as in being the only gallery that showcases her work. I want her here in New York."

I need time to prepare her for something like this. But will the offer still be on the table if she drags her heels? "When can you be here?"

"For her? In a couple of days. Just tell me the time and place."

"How about I check to see when she's free, then text the meeting details?"

After hanging up with Andrés, I try to figure a way to

make this meeting happen, knowing it won't be an easy sell.

"Is this the surprise you were referring to? Please say it isn't. Please say this guy isn't coming here to meet me."

"Ragan, what's the big deal?" I ask, knowing this is a *huge* fucking deal. "Just sit and talk to the guy. Can't hurt to hear him out."

"I can't do this. I won't. Now stop trying to push me to do things that aren't in me to do."

I've argued with Ragan for the better part of an hour now, and I'm starting to lose my patience. "If it's not in you, then how the fuck did you paint these?" I walk over and lift one of the drawings from the corner. "Do you think just *anyone* can do this? I sure as hell can't. Andrés says you have a natural talent, like none he's ever seen. Or do you think he's lying too?"

She storms out of the room, but with no intention of letting this go, I follow her.

"I still can't believe you did this behind my back. I knew you and Dad were up to something. He's *never* taken an interest in anything about me."

"He's way past due, don't you think? Maybe he was finally trying to help."

Ragan spins around to face me, outraged by my claim. "Help? Are you kidding me? He doesn't give a damn. He never has. So, tell me, when you and he were having these secret meetings, did he happen to mention that he once tossed my art out of the house like it was garbage?"

"He did what?" I ask, my eyes moving over her in confusion.

"Never mind. I'm not in the mood for a stroll down memory lane."

"You don't want to talk about it, fine. But you need to meet with this guy."

"I don't *need* to do anything, Branch. I'm tired of being pushed around, okay? People have been pushing me into things with force or with subtle ways of mind control for years and I'm not letting it happen anymore. You need to go."

"I'm not moving. Not until you tell me you're going to do this."

"Well, you're going to have a long wait. I'm not doing it. I can't."

"Why do you keep saying that?"

"Because I can't afford to get caught up in what-if's. I've done that one time too many, and look where it's gotten me. And now, I have a child to think about, not these pie-in-the-sky dreams. Everyone can't be like you."

The mere thought of her diminishing herself because of that loser ex makes me see red, and a flare of anger touches my chest. "This is your ex talking. Isn't it? Whatever load of bull he dumped on you, don't buy into that shit. You deserve so much better than what you've had to deal with. You know that…don't you? What happened to that strong-willed girl that doesn't take any crap from me?"

"Even the strongest of winds can turn and even the strongest of glass can shatter. And sometimes when enough becomes enough, that's exactly what happens."

"Why the defeatist attitude, Ragan? I expect that from some people, but not you. Why are you so convinced your dreams can't come true?"

"Because I tried! Okay. I tried!"

She goes to the closet and pulls out two canvas pieces and tosses them at me.

"Now tell me if that looks like talent to you," she demands. "Yesterday when you told me about all of this, I'll admit, for a few minutes, I was excited. I allowed myself to dream. So I pulled out my supplies and this is what came of it."

I pick up the drawings, instantly determining they pay no resemblance to what I've seen of her work, not even to that I'd witnessed her scribbling in passing at the diner.

"Are you happy now?" she asks.

I glance up from the paintings and see her eyes glistening with tears. "Ragan, you've let that fucking guy get in your head. This is what he wants—for you to give up on yourself. Don't let him win. You're better than this."

She shakes her head. "No. I'm not. I thought I was. I really did. But this is as good as it's gonna get for me, Branch. I have to accept that. And so do you. Stop filling my head with these pipe dreams of a life that's meant for someone else. Now please, go."

"You know, I never pegged you for a quitter. That sure is a lot for Cecelia to live up to."

Her head flicks around. "How dare you say that shit to me! Do you have any idea what I've had to survive? Of the number of times I thought I was going to die because the person who was *supposed* to love me beat the living shit out of me until she was too fucking tired to lift her arm or her foot? Of knowing I have a mother out there who never gave a damn about me, who chose drugs over me?"

Enraged by my accusation, both her voice and her temper

escalate with each word.

"What about the number of self-talks I give myself on a daily basis just so I can keep putting one foot in front of the other? Do you know about that? Do you? Don't bother answering because I know you don't. Unlike you, I don't get to walk off into some high-profile fantasy life and just come back here and slum it up when the mood strikes. I'm here every day. Every fucking day, surrounded by shit that hits me with every memory I try to forget. With everything I try *not* to expose my daughter to. So don't you fucking dare stand here and call me a fucking quitter."

"Ragan—"

"Get out! Get out!"

Her hands come up to shove me, but my position is unyielding, not swaying an inch. Then with an unharnessed fervor she pounds my chest, her fists striking me repeatedly as she shouts for me to leave.

I grasp her wrists. "Stop it, Ragan. Stop it. I'm sorry."

"Go. Just go," she weeps, her energy waning as she falls into me and surrenders to the emotion that's taken its hold. I wrap my arms around her, letting her release it all, her shoulders shaking and her body vibrating as my chest swallows her sobs.

Her cries are painful to hear. They're cries of a woman who's tired of fighting the fight only to be knocked down... the cries of a woman drained of all hope.

Chapter
TWENTY-SEVEN

Ragan

S ITTING IN JIM BOB'S ON MY LUNCH BREAK, I FILL
Hayley in on Branch's crusade to launch my art career.
Something I never considered—something I never
thought plausible. She's the only other person, besides my
dad, Noah, and Ethan who know of my drawings. She, like
Branch, has always encouraged me to do something with it.
But nothing as life-altering as what Branch has initiated.

"I told you before, Branch really likes you, Ragan,"
Hayley says, a big smile on her face. "I can see it when he
looks at you. And he's done so many things to prove it. He
really cares for you. Why would he go through all of this if
he didn't?"

"Did I hear you right?"

I look up to see the mean-girl bitchy face of Skye
Jamison. This diner is bringing in all types since word of it
being Branch's lunch spot has spread around town, which
is one reason he doesn't come by as much anymore. "We

actually weren't speaking to you, so if you heard anything, you were eavesdropping."

"Yeah, nosey much," Hayley adds.

She casts an upturned nose in my best friend's direction. "Do you *ever* have any business of your own, or are you too busy in Ragan's?"

"This isn't high school where you can toss out your little burns and wait on your bitch crew to back you up. So keep it up, Skye. I'm pretty sure I can break you in half."

"Hayley, don't waste your time on this one," I say, instantly heated by the memory of her mouth on Branch. "She's not worth it."

"Excuse me?" She looks as if I shouldn't have the audacity to respond to her. "Ragan, please. Just because Branch has thrown a little pity your way, don't think you're any more than you've ever been. Actually you've slid even further down the totem pole."

"So this is about Branch and how he continues to reject you," I snap back. "There's a little something called pride, Skye. Maybe you should try to scrape up some."

"*Pride*? You should look into that yourself, sweetheart. If you think you're anything more than a pity fuck for Branch, you're out of your mind. You don't seriously think he wants you, do you?"

I look at Hayley and then back at Skye.

"Oh? So you did? Ragan, Ragan, Ragan. Bless your heart," she says, her tone condescending. "Look at you. You're a waitress for God's sake. So you've lost some weight. Doesn't change who you are under that tacky uniform, my dear. An undereducated reject with a kid. What could Branch McGuire possibly see in someone like *you*? Especially when he can have someone like me?"

"I'm betting he sees a heck of a lot more in Ragan than he does in a person as vile as you," Jim Bob pipes in from out of nowhere, a distasteful grimace on his face as he eyes Skye.

Her mouth falls open, her eyes wide with shock.

"Didn't your parents ever teach you any manners? You should be ashamed of yourself. To say such nasty things to someone as good as Ragan. You'd do good to be half the person she is one day."

"I don't think this is any of your concern. Besides I'm a *customer* and I demand you show me some respect."

"Well, you aren't the kind of customer I want, so I *demand* you get the hell out of here."

When Skye realizes Jim Bob means business, she turns on a heel with a huff and stalks out of the diner.

Paying no more attention to Satan's Mistress, my gaze flies back to my boss. I thought he only saw me as a mess of an employee he'd been coerced into keeping on the payroll.

"What?" he asks, taking in my bewildered expression. "A man can't speak up when he sees someone's being mistreated?"

"It's not that. I just didn't think—"

"You didn't deserve any of that," he says. "You're a good seed, Ragan."

I smile broadly and say, "Thank you, Jim Bob."

"Now don't go getting all bubbly, because although you're a good seed, you're a crummy waitress."

Hayley doubles over in laughter as my boss waddles off. I can't help but smile myself. But it's short-lived as I think back to Skye's description of me. That can't be how Branch sees me. Or can it?

"Ragan."

I turn in the direction of the small voice and spot a woman standing near the side of the diner. I think I recognize her, then I question if I really do. "Do I know you?"

She takes a few steps toward me and on instinct, I do the opposite.

A shameful smile thins her lips. "You should, but it's my fault that you don't."

She steps from the shadows and although she looks different—older and a lot worse for wear—I do know who she is. And the shock of seeing her only a few feet away has paralyzed both my legs and my vocal cords.

She brushes a hand over her brittle hair, a futile effort to tidy her appearance. "I can see from your expression that you know who I am."

Yeah, I know who the fuck you are and I have no desire to see or talk to you. All the words I've wanted to say for years, all the words I should say are stuck in my throat. And that's probably best because they would be wasted on the likes of her. Bolting from my stupor, I spin around and head for my car.

"Ragan. Please wait."

She calls after me but my steps quicken as I try to place distance between myself and the woman who gave me life.

I reach my car and open the door, anxious to get the hell away from the egg donor who's never deserved the title of mother. But then she ends me with her next four words.

"He's not your father."

My head whips up and I whirl around to face her, the brown of my eyes meeting the same brown of hers. Obviously she wants my attention, and now she has it. "What did you say?"

She takes a deep breath as if summoning her courage. And then on an exhale, she repeats, "David Prescott isn't your father."

My eyes crawl over her, rage gripping me as I stare at the woman who's apparently hell bent on ruining what little is left of Ragan Prescott. "What the hell are you talking about? Of course he's my father. Why would you say something like that?"

She rubs her hand up and down her arm as if something's there that shouldn't be. "Because it's true. I mean, yes, he's the man who raised you, but you're not his…not biologically."

"If your plan was to come here and tell lies on top of everything else you've done to fuck up my life, then you need to turn around and crawl back into whatever drug-infested hole you came from."

My words do much to deliver the slap across her face she deserves. But she doesn't move. She stands in place, her eyes locked on mine.

"It's the truth, Ragan. When I met your dad, I was a mess. Doing just about anything to get my next hit," she says, scratching a hand over her nose.

From the looks of it, she's still as big of a mess now as she was then. She takes a step closer and the soft breeze brings her stench to my nose. I look her over. Her shirt reveals several days' worth of stains, paired with pants that are two-to-three sizes too large, secured at her waist by a ripped cloth. And it looks as if she's missing at least two of her front teeth. The ones that remain look as though they haven't seen a toothbrush in ages. My stomach cringes. I don't understand how I could have been born to a woman like her.

"But when I met David, for some reason, he saw something in me." A frail smile morphs her features and for a flicker of a second, I can see she was once a beautiful woman.

"I was havin' some money problems 'round that time. Lost my apartment. Was livin' in my car for 'bout two months. Cleanin' myself up whenever I could…at restaurants, retail stores, even the car wash. I'd scored some cash one night doin' things I'm embarrassed to even say, but it was enough to get a motel for a week. It wasn't much but I was out of my car, so hey, that's a win, right?"

I don't remember her voice being so southern. Then again, I don't remember her voice at all. She shrugs and lifts her brows as if awaiting my agreement. When I don't respond, she continues.

"It was my last night at the Fleetwood Inn and I wanted to do somethin' special for myself. There wasn't a lot of money left so I got all dressed up and treated myself to a night out. I had dinner at one of those fancy restaurants I'd always wanted to go to and then after that, I went to this dive bar on the outskirts of town. And there he was. Your father. We got to talkin' and we really hit it off. He asked to see me the next day. And the next. By then I was back in my car."

Dad never told me any of this, so I can't really say if it's the truth or not. And even though I don't want to hear anymore, I listen. I take in every word.

"We dated for 'bout a month. Hardly a day went by that we didn't see each other. He was always so kind to me. Seeing things in me that I knew weren't really there. He used to say I was special…his special angel…that's what he called me." She falls quiet, seemingly reminiscent as her gaze drops to her battered sneakers. Then, exhaling a sigh, she lifts her eyes to mine. "He eventually learned the truth—that I was down on my luck. He didn't know 'bout the other part…the drugs. And for a while, things were good. I mean, better than I thought I'd ever have with anyone. Then I got sick. Ended up in the emergency room and found out I was pregnant. David did the math. Knew it wasn't his, but he wanted to be with me and he wanted to raise you as his own." She lifts her shoulders in a shrug. "And who was I to refuse somethin' like that? A few years later, I had your brother. Then some months passed and I ran into the gang I used to party with. It wasn't long before I fell off the wagon. Started usin' again. I tried to hide it," she says, stroking her nose like the cocaine addicts I'd seen in the movies. "But David recognized the signs. He tried to convince me to get help, but I refused. I didn't have the strength to do it. He eventually gave me an ultimatum."

I dislodge the lump in my throat. "And you chose the drugs."

She struggles with what to say, her mouth opening and closing, her gaze wandering my face as she fights for the words. "I didn't choose the drugs, Ragan. They chose me."

I shake my head disgusted by both her and her story. "The addict's motto. What a load of bull." I have the sudden urge to punch her. To keep punching her until all of my pain is gone. But no amount of punching would ever eradicate the ache that sits with me every day. I choke back the rage that threatens to take its hold and I glare at the person who gave me birth. The woman who brought me into this world only to leave me.

And then for some asinine reason, she steps even closer and reaches out to me.

I take a few steps back. "Don't ever touch me." The hatred I thought I felt for her is nothing compared to what I feel as I look at her now. She's a lying, used-up, pathetic excuse for a mother. And she's never served a purpose in my life unless you count her as being my ongoing representation of what *not* to be. Then out of nowhere, she shows up. And for what? To tear me into even smaller pieces with her lies? What kind of person does that?

I remain firmly implanted, a few feet away from her, warring with myself and barely containing what I've only dreamt of unleashing. She's a liar. She's an addict. And she's a waste of humanity. I rake my eyes over her, questioning why. Why is she doing this? What does she want from me? A thank-you? Money? A relationship? None of that will ever happen. She has to know that. So why bother with this crap? Unless... unless she *is* telling the truth? What if David Prescott isn't my father? Is that why it was so easy for him to let Cassidy torture and degrade me? Is that the reason I was never truly loved by either of them? And it's that logic that fuels my next question.

"If the man who raised me isn't my father...who is?"

Our eyes hold.

My chest constricts as I await her reply.

And something that resembles shame washes over her face when she finally answers, "I don't know."

Chapter
TWENTY-EIGHT

Branch

"**C**OME IN," I SAY, SHOCKED TO SEE HER AT MY front door given the way our last quarrel ended. "Thank you," she replies, and follows me to the living room.

I sit on the couch and she assumes the chair across from me. To break the silence, I ask, "Can I grab you something to drink?"

She looks up at me and shakes her head. "He told me all these things so that I could be the person he wanted me to be."

First I'm confused but then I realize, she's ready to talk about Ethan. About what he'd done to her. So I sit back and listen.

"And I didn't know it then, but I know now. It made me resentful. It made me angry. And that's why I was always so defensive and sullen with you. I think I started to think that men wanted to use me and treat me however they wanted and then expect me to just take it. That's what he'd convinced me of. And that's what I'd become for him. I was his own special version of what he thought I should be. I fell at his feet and treated him like a god. And when I stopped doing that, everything changed—a different Ethan surfaced. When I finally got up the courage to leave, I told myself, no more. After Cassidy and then Ethan, I was done. I was determined to stand up for myself at all costs, even at times when it really wasn't necessary."

She sits on the edge of the chair, her fingers twisting in her lap. And then all of a sudden, she speaks, adding more detail to her story. "Over the years, he somehow usurped every ounce of my independence and my pride. I felt as if I was nothing without him. And that's what he wanted. That's how he made me feel. He would sometimes even say it aloud when he saw even a tiny glimmer of spirit in me. He said I would never have a better life than the one I had with him. That I'd never have anyone half as good as him and that people like you would overlook me or treat me like I was a scrap of garbage. I think when you hear that type of thing for so long, you start to believe it. Between him and Cassidy, and how they degraded me, it's a wonder I had the will to get out of bed every day."

"He's a piece of shit, Ragan."

She meets my eyes. "I know that now. And I'm sorry for giving you such a hard time. You've been more to me in these last few months than anyone has been for me in my entire life. You made me feel worthy and you gave me hope. You've protected me, defended me, taken care of me…and my daughter. And the only thing you've asked for in return is for me to be my best self."

I see how difficult this is for her, but I'm glad she's opening up. It means she's ready to move on from the dark cloud of her past. "So is this what you came by to tell me?"

"Yeah. And to say thank you for removing my last obstacle."

My brows scrunch.

"I got the papers—only allowing Ethan supervised visitation. I don't know how you pulled it off, but I owe you big."

"I was shooting for no visitation at all but that didn't pan out, but if he missteps just once, we've got him. He's out of your life for good."

"He'll mess up. It's in him. He won't be able to help himself."

She looks around the room, as if she wants to say more but doesn't know if she should. When she finally parts her lips to speak, loud rock music blasts through the speaker system.

"Jace has some friends over," I explain. "The music is supposed to be focused in the game room, but I don't think he quite understands how to work the control system. Let's go to the porch."

Once I'm outside standing in front of her, I ask, "So how are the paintings coming along?"

She gives me a shy smile. "I guess you heard, huh?"

"Yeah."

"So he made me an offer."

"And?"

"I don't know what to do."

"Why? It's a no-brainer, Ragan."

"Yeah, maybe for you, but…"

"But what?"

Heat rises to her cheeks and her eyes leave mine. With her gaze resting at my chest, she says, "I feel like for the first time in my life, I have someone on my side. Someone who's willing to fight for me even when I've done my damnedest to push that someone away."

I want to pull her in my arms, but I resist the urge. "That someone will always be on your side, no matter how many miles are between you and that someone."

"Maybe," she says, finally looking back up at me. "But it won't be the same."

"I want you to go."

The sadness in her expression deepens. For long seconds, she stares at me, the light in her eyes starting to fade. I see what my words do to her but I can't be selfish and ask her to stay.

"But what about you?" she finally asks.

I grasp her hand and we take a seat on the steps, just like we did at my childhood home. "I suppose I'll be here. Besides, you're ready to stand on your own. You don't need me anymore."

"I never *needed* you. But it was good to have you around… just in case I did."

"You have to do what's best for you and your daughter," I say, although I want to swallow each one of those words. "And Blue Ridge isn't it."

She lets out a long sigh. "I guess I have some thinking to do. I just wanted to come by and personally say thanks for all you've done for me."

She reaches over to pull me into a hug. And when she releases me, a feeling of loss curls in my stomach. Although I know the move is what's best, all I can think is I don't want to see her go.

Chapter
TWENTY-NINE

Branch

I'M SITTING ON THE PORCH WHEN RAGAN PULLS UP. I watch as she slides out of the car and makes her way to the front of the house. She has a confidence in her step that wasn't visible even a few weeks ago, and I immediately notice the feeling that gives me. I'm proud of her. But there's something else…that unrecognizable emotion that always seems to surface when I think of her. It's a feeling I don't quite understand, so as usual, I push it aside.

"I've decided to do it," she says, when she reaches me. "CeeCee and I are moving to New York."

I step down from the porch, pick her up and twirl her around. Her arms fly around my neck and her laughter fills the air. It's a sweet sound that brings a smile to my lips. I set her down on her feet and say, "I knew you'd make the right decision."

A wide smile crinkles the corners of her eyes. "I can't believe I'm doing this."

"I hope you're ready for your life to change in a major way because it's about to."

"That's what Andrés keeps repeating…almost verbatim. I think he's more excited than I am."

"What does Cecelia think?"

"As much as any kid her age can, I suppose."

"I know you were worried about how the move would affect her but she'll be fine."

"I'm starting to think you're right. Since the court orders don't place any limitations on my place of residence, there's nothing holding me back. So if I'm going to do this, now is the right time. She's not in school yet, so she won't be leaving any friends behind, and Lord knows it's good to place a few hundred miles between her and my joke of a family."

I look straight into her eyes. She's different. A striking dissimilarity to the sullen waitress I'd met at the diner. "I'm proud of you."

As she studies my face, her smile slowly vanishes. "Then why don't you look like it?"

I shrug. "I don't know. I guess I'm gonna miss you."

"What?" She feigns a shocked expression.

"I know. Surprises the hell out of me, too."

I know she sees it in my eyes. I *really* am gonna miss her. And I wonder if it's even a fraction of the amount I know she'll miss me.

She waves me off. "Eh…you'll move on to your next charity project in no time."

My brow arches. "Is that what you think you are to me?"

She looks away, unwilling to respond to a question I sense she already knows the answer to.

"You know," she says, changing the subject. "I'll bet you

fall in love, get married and stay right here in Blue Ridge."

I let out a cynical laugh. "That's a bet you'll lose, so save all those big bucks you'll be making."

"You really don't think love is in the cards for you?"

I shake my head. "Nope."

"Have you ever been in love or had a girlfriend?"

"There was one. Madison. I mentioned her to you before."

"What happened? Did she dump you?" she asks, her mouth twisting into a mocking smile.

"According to her, the longer I was away, the more she faded to the back of my thoughts…until I eventually stopped thinking about her altogether."

"Was she right?"

I shrug and guide her to sit beside me in the swing. "I didn't think so at the time, but I guess I get it now."

"What changed your mind?"

"More like *who*. It was Jimmy. I've never seen a man more in love or who doted on any woman the way he did Loretta. He once told me he knew she was the one because every single day, regardless of who he was with or what he was doing, she consumed his every thought. Of all the girls he'd dated, she was the one he couldn't get out of his head—the one he couldn't stop thinking about."

"To be the object of that kind of affection, it must have been an amazing love affair. I guess when you think about it, that's all any girl wants—to be the one her guy can't stop thinking about. That's when you'll know."

"Know what?"

"That he's forever."

"Forever, huh?" I shake my head. "I don't know if I can be that."

"I think you'll get there."

My brow lifts. "I don't know why you'd think that."

"Because of what you've done for me. And because of what I said a while back…I see a change in you. You may not notice it right off, but you aren't the same arrogant dick that stepped into Jim Bob's a few months ago. I think losing Jimmy, seeing your mom go through one of her more intense mental breaks, reconnecting with your family and accepting what you need to be to Jace and to Jimmy's family…all of that has changed you. I think you want more than you've ever wanted in the past."

"So not only are you a soon-to-be world-renowned artist but you dabble in psychology, too."

"Oh, whatever."

She leans into me, placing her head on my shoulder. Being close to her like this…the comfort I have with her, that she has with me, it feels…right.

"So have you stepped inside your childhood home yet?" she asks.

"Nope. Told you I wasn't doing that."

"Why buy that place if you have no intention of going in?"

"As a reminder of what I don't want."

"I'll bet it's more than that."

"You'd lose *that* bet, too."

"Then prove me wrong. Go inside. Face it. Let it wash over you. Let it cleanse you, then you can move on."

"Ragan, drop it, all right."

She looks up at me. "It's what made you who you are, so accept it. That's what I did. It was hard. I cried a lot but I finally faced it, and in the end I'm better for it. I think you will be, too. Maybe once you finally face the last bit of hurt and pain of your past, you'll be able to let that girl in."

"What girl?"

"The one *you* can't stop thinking about."

Her brown eyes linger in mine and I absentmindedly touch a finger to her cheek. I'd pulled her from a broken place and now she's trying to do the same for me. "I'm not Jimmy. That was *his* life. That will never be me."

"It's like talking to a brick wall. Maybe you're right. Maybe this is all you want or will ever be. Such a waste." She exhales a sigh. "I suppose I should get going. I only wanted to drop by and give you the news…and to say thank you…again."

"I didn't do anything, but give you a hard time."

"You did far more than that and you know it."

"This is for you," she says and passes me the box she'd been holding.

"And here I am without anything to give to you," I joke, grinning as I remove the ribbon.

"No," she says. "Wait and open it later."

"Er…okay," I say, looking up from the box.

She exhales a long sigh. "I hate to rush off but Carrie, Patty, and Hayley are taking me out for a going away dinner."

We get up from the swing and take the walk to her car.

"Remember to call if you need anything," I say, when I open the door for her.

"I will."

She looks up at me from under her lashes and I swear I see her eyes water. Before I can say anything she reaches up to hug me, then tugs me toward her and kisses my cheek. "Take care of yourself, Branch."

"You, too, Ragan."

I stand in the street long after she's gone, seeing nothing and wishing I'd kissed her—I mean *really* kissed her. I exhale a sigh and head back up the walkway, then grab the box from the swing before stepping back into the house.

I go to the game room and grab a beer from the mini-fridge, plop down in one of the game chairs, then turn on the TV. I pick up Ragan's box from the table, shuffling it from one hand to the other a few times before my curiosity gets the better of me.

Removing the lid, I find the contents wrapped in white tissue, which I quickly snatch and toss on the floor. I lift the gift from the box and my lips curve into a smile. It's something she'd drawn and framed. It's a picture from *that* night. The night I'd taken something from her. Something I don't remember.

The image in the frame is a depiction of me on the night of our homecoming. The 2001 Dawson versus Blue Ridge banner is in the background, and I'm standing on the football field with my helmet in one hand and a football in the other.

She'd finally used representational art in one of her paintings. I sit back, shocked that she'd taken my advice. I shake my head, then flip the frame over to pull out the flap and spot a note.

That night was not a mistake. And if it was…it's the
best one I ever made.
Ragan

Chapter
THIRTY

Ragan

T HE DAY ANGIE PRESCOTT SAID SHE DIDN'T KNOW
who my father was could've been the final blow
that crushed me whole. And had it not been for the
positive force Branch had become in my life, it very well may
have sent me spiraling.

I could have confronted David, and I could have launched
a search for a man I'd never find but I didn't see the point in
doing either. It wouldn't change anything about my past and
it would only serve to muddy my present.

That evening after having seen Angie, I walked into my
home just as I had the previous nights. When CeeCee was
fast asleep, I went to my room and flipped off the lights. Then
I lay in bed and traced my life from birth till present day.
And that's when I finally decided I'd had enough of the bad.
It was time for the good.

"So you're finally getting out of here?" Dad asks.

"Yeah. I think it's time. It's past time actually. There's nothing for me here except a lot of shit I want to forget."

His lips fall into a frown. "You mean me?"

"My life has been hell, and it's mostly because you allowed it to be, so yeah."

"I did the best I could."

I shake my head. "If that was your best, I guess I'd be dead if you hadn't tried at all."

"Ragan, I know you will never understand but I did try."

"No. You didn't. You gave up."

"I never should have invited Cassidy into our lives," he says, the stain of guilt coloring his expression. "But I was trying to make up for what you didn't have. I was trying to give you a mother."

"But you let her beat us. You sat by and watched. Every day. How could you do that?"

His shoulders gradually slide into a slump but he quickly recovers. "I guess I figured having a piece of a mother was better than having no mother at all."

"You figured wrong, Dad. And Noah...you never gave him a second thought when he ran away. That can't be your idea of *trying*. All you've done is given us three parental figures we'll have to fight like hell to forget."

"Well, I did do that part right."

My brows scrunch. "What are you talking about?"

"I kept Angie out of your life."

We never said my mother's name aloud. *Ever.* "How did you do that?"

"Three years after she left, I received a call from her asking to come home."

His words catch me off guard. "She came back to Blue Ridge?"

"No. She was in Montgomery, and I didn't want to risk her coming here, so I went there. She'd tried her best to clean herself up, to make herself look presentable but I saw enough to know she was still using. The only reason she called me is because she'd hit rock bottom again and had no one else to turn to. Her intent was obvious. She wanted me to bail her out, just as I'd done in the past. When she realized I wasn't buying into her sob story, she chose to barter sexual favors in exchange for money. I was disgusted by it all, so I left her at that seedy motel, hightailed it back here and blocked the entire episode out of my head."

I stare at him, unable to process my thoughts. With a loss for words, I drop to the chair behind me and my eyes fall to the smudge of dirt on the carpet. Once Dad's revelation runs its course, I lift my gaze to his. "You don't think I deserved to know this before now?"

"For what Ragan? To make your life even worse?"

"Maybe seeing her children would have helped."

"She left two toddlers behind. Do you honestly believe she would've thought twice about doing the same to two grade-school kids?"

I know he's right, but I still should have known. Maybe, just maybe, it would have made a difference.

"She was a mess. It was several degrees worse than it had *ever* been before," he replies, justifying his decision. "I didn't want her anywhere near you or your brother."

"And Cassidy was so much better?"

"At the time I thought so."

"Well, you thought wrong! I'm all kinds of fucked up

because of you and that woman."

He closes the distance between us. "Ragan, don't say that."

"Why not? It's true. My entire life has been one cruel-ass joke. I was born a crack baby with a crap load of immune issues, abandoned by my mother, beaten within an inch of my life for most of my childhood and I'm the single mom of a child who has a horrible father. Everything about my life up until now has left me scarred and drowning in all sorts of insecurities I fight every day to keep buried."

"Ragan, I didn't—"

"Save it, Dad," I cut him off and start toward the door. "I may be in touch one of these days." I turn back, my hand already on the door knob, and take one last look at the man who may or may not be my father. "Then again, maybe I won't."

After a tearless farewell to David Prescott, my daughter and I meet Hayley for a celebratory goodbye brunch. She makes repeated offers to drive us to the airport but that will more than likely end with a tearfully snotty send-off that neither of us will easily walk away from. She asks about Branch and I tell her we said our goodbyes a couple of days ago. And although he, too, offered to drive us to the airport, I declined his offer as well.

Other than *odd*, I don't have a label for my relationship with Branch but I know I'll miss whatever it is, and despite our agreement to keep in touch, the chances of me seeing him ever again are next to zero. To be honest, I want to squeeze in those final moments with Branch but spending any more time with him will make the goodbye that much harder.

A few hours later, with only one piece of luggage, my child and I board a first class flight to New York City. Andrés and his assistant Autumn made the move from Georgia pretty much seamless. There was very little packing to do because the plan was to leave the majority of our clothing behind. But as I'd pulled the items from my closet, I couldn't help but picture the grimy image of my mother and it reminded me of so many others who were in similar situations—homeless and in need of clean clothes. Not that they were of much value, but I donated everything other than a couple days' worth of clothing to the women and children's shelter. That left me with only one bag to pack for us. Everything else—new wardrobes, airfare, a loft apartment, childcare, and transportation—had all been arranged.

I'm anxious to get settled in my new place. When Autumn emailed the video tour of it, I couldn't believe my eyes. It's an amazing space—already furnished with items that appear too fancy to touch, let alone use or sit on. The kitchen pantries are chock-full of food and our closets are jam-packed with clothes. There's literally nothing left for me to do except step into our new lives.

It's all too good to be true—that's what I keep telling myself. I'm actually still waiting to awaken from the wild and crazy dream because no way can this be my life. Ragan Prescott, courted and wooed by one of the most widely acclaimed art gallery owners. Now here I am, moving to the cultural, financial, and media capital of the world, and set up like a celebrity. Life has offered me a dream so far beyond my expectations that it doesn't seem real. Maybe I should pinch myself and wake up before this gets any better. Things like this just don't happen to people like me.

But somehow it has.

And now to prove to Andrés, Branch, and most importantly to myself, that their belief in me is not misplaced.

Chapter
THIRTY-ONE

Branch

"THE TOWN COUNCIL CHAIRMAN CALLED THIS morning. He said you donated the remaining funds to complete the project."

"Yeah, I did. He wanted to be the one to tell you the news."

"Thank you, Branch. It meant a lot to Jimmy. He really wanted these kids to have something special. Something to keep them out of trouble and to fuel their creativity."

"That's why I had to see it finished," I reply, then imagine the look on Jimmy's face.

"I've gotta say, I was surprised by the name. I can't believe they agreed to that."

"Money talks. Besides, everyone loved Jimmy. The decision was unanimous."

"*The Perez-McGuire Academic Recreational Center.* That has a nice ring to it," Loretta says. "He wasn't one for having a light shined his way, but he would have loved being a part of this. And the dedication's next week?"

"Tuesday at eleven. I'll be there."

"So you're really gonna stick around here?"

"As much as I can in the off-season."

She waggles her brows. "I'm guessing a certain waitress and her little girl are very excited about that."

"And that's where you'd be wrong."

Loretta's smile all but disappears. "What have you done? Don't tell me you've pushed her away again with that pompous celebrity playboy act of yours."

"Not this time," I say, with a faux grin. "They moved to New York."

"New York?" she echoes.

"Yeah, they left a couple of days ago." I pull Ragan's note from my pocket. "She asked me to give you this."

Loretta's brows scrunch as she reaches for the envelope. "Can you hold L.J. for a sec?"

Having gotten pretty comfortable with the little guy, I lift him from her arms and hold him out in front of me. "Hey there, L.J. How's my little buddy doing?"

"So she's gone?" Loretta asks, looking up from the letter.

"Yep," I reply, hoping she doesn't see how Ragan's departure has gotten under my skin.

Her lips curve into a frown as her gaze skates over my face. "Oh, Branch. I'm sorry."

Apparently my efforts are wasted because she sees right through my act, but I still play it off. "Sorry for what? This is a once-in-a-lifetime opportunity for her."

"I agree. It's amazing. But you miss her, don't you?"

"Who?"

"The person we're talking about. The person you always seem to bring into our conversations lately."

"Nah, I'm good. She became a friend. We had some fun, but that's about it. You know I'm not looking for anything else."

"Just because you weren't looking doesn't mean you didn't find it."

I shrug. "I *do* miss Cecelia." I look down at the baby and grab his tiny hand. "I guess I miss her mom a little, too."

Loretta's smiling at me when I finally glance up from L.J.

"What's with the look?" I ask.

"Our little Branch has finally fallen in love."

"Not funny, Loretta. You know that isn't me."

"Jimmy called it, you know," she says, continuing as if she's uncovered some mystery.

"Called what?"

"You and Ragan. He really liked her. Thought she was good for you. He said she'd be the girl you'd marry."

My brows shoot up. "*Marry.* You do realize you're talking to Branch McGuire, right?"

"I'm sure that's what you want me to believe. And it's probably what you're trying to convince yourself of but no, I'm *not* talking to that arrogant guy you show to the world. I'm talking to the man I've considered family for the last umpteen years. I know you, Branch. And Jimmy knew you better, so I'm pretty sure he called it right."

"Nah. Jimmy wouldn't say anything crazy like that. He knew I wasn't the settling-down type. Hell, the whole world knows. Especially not with someone like Ragan."

She crosses her arms over her chest and angles her head. "And what's wrong with Ragan?"

"I didn't say anything was *wrong* with her but you've seen the kind of girls I hook up with. Ragan's not my type."

"Or maybe *those* girls weren't your type, which is why they've all been easy to walk away from."

I shake my head in denial. "Look, Loretta, I don't have a thing for Ragan."

She reaches for the baby and says, "You don't have to pretend with me, you know. Or maybe…"

"Maybe what?"

"Maybe you don't realize it yourself. But I can see it. Jimmy saw it coming, too. Even Isidora and Luciana asked me about it the day after we were all out on the lake."

"Like I said, we've become good friends. An unlikely coupling, but still, good friends. And I want what's best for her. To see her happy. I hardly think that equates jumping the broom or anything close to it."

"Didn't you say you had an offer to play with the New York Cyclops?" she asks, still pushing her agenda.

"Yeah, but I'm planning to sign with the Atlanta Eagles to stay closer to Mama, Jace, Dad, and you guys."

"Your mama is better than she's been in years. She has Curtis. And I'm getting better every day. We'll always be family. And we'll always look out for one another. Mary, Curtis, Jace, me, my girls, and Little Jimmy. We're family. And family looks out for family, so we'll all be fine. You need to live your life."

"That's what I've been doing for the last sixteen years. I need to finally accept that I have responsibilities."

"Like your mama, Jace, and the garage?"

"Well…yeah."

"I've given this a great deal of thought, and I believe Jimmy left that to you because he figured it would be a while before you found anyone who'd take you," she laughs. "And on a more serious note, he knew it held special memories for the both of you. You don't have to live *here* for that garage to belong to you."

I consider Loretta's words and my chest clenches. "I still can't believe he's gone. I walk in there every day expecting to see him leaning over the hood of a car."

"I know what you mean. I reach for him in bed at night or I walk in the kitchen looking for him at the counter holding that World's Greatest Dad mug."

"The blue one with the chip and the glued handle?" I ask, with a chuckle.

"That's the one. Tater was three years old and she was so excited to bring that Father's Day gift to Papi. She ran into the room that morning, holding it out to him. But she tripped and fell just before she made it to the bed. And when Jimmy opened the box, the handle was broken and a small piece had chipped from the rim. Tater cried and cried, but her dad told her it was okay, that he could reattach the handle and that he would love it even more because it would have character."

Loretta's eyes glaze over and dense silence fills the room.

She finally looks down at L.J. lying quietly in her arms and I stare at the two of them wishing like hell Jimmy could be here with his wife and son.

"Jimmy would want you to go after her," she says, lifting her gaze to mine. "To forget about the garage. You'd have his blessing…and mine."

"Loretta, I can't do that."

"You *can*. My brother-in-law Alejandro is coming down next month. He's moving the family here. After losing Jimmy, he's decided he wants to be closer to us. You can hire him as the general manager and he can report to you periodically."

I take in her earnest expression, my elbows resting on my knees as I lean forward. "I can't back out on Jimmy's last request of me. Not after all he's meant to my life."

"Jimmy would be so proud of you for stepping in to help us, but he'd tell you to go. Branch, you know that, don't you?"

"Loretta, I appreciate what you're trying to do here, but my mind is made up. I'm staying."

She shakes her head, her lips pressing into a thin line. "Okay, but if you change your mind..."

"I won't."

Chapter
THIRTY-TWO

Branch

I T WAS A SMALL CEREMONY AT THE HOUSE. THE MARRIAGE wasn't actually necessary since they never divorced, therefore, it was more of a symbolic gesture for Jace, Dad, Mama, and me—somewhat of a reset. A new beginning for the McGuires.

Mama was over the moon when I finally came around to accepting this new normal. A large part of my lowered resistance was Jimmy. He would have insisted that I—at the very least—give it a try. All the time and effort he'd poured into me can't have been for naught and if nothing else, his death made me realize it was past time I grew the fuck up.

And Mama—well more so Jace—made me see how this *new family* could actually be a good thing. Still not one hundred percent convinced though, I spent some time with Mama's psychiatrist Dr. Blake who suggested we schedule routine sessions to iron out some unresolved issues and to also form an action plan—something we desperately need if our family is to function as a healthy unit. So after weeks of therapy, I gave Dad what he asked for—my blessing.

I've never seen Mama smile or laugh as much since I was a kid. She was *happy* and she wanted the wedding to be a family affair which meant the four of us planned it all. We each had to add something unique to the ceremony and everyone did, including me, with a lot of help from Nurse Christina.

And when the big day came, I walked Mama down the aisle and gave her back to the man she's always belonged to— my dad, Curtis McGuire. When I placed Mama's hand in his, it felt right. It felt permanent.

As they recited their vows, I realized that as children, we mistakenly hold our parents to a higher standard than we do ourselves but truth is, they are just like the kids, making mistakes and learning as they go. So yes, my parents could have handled several things very differently, especially Dad, but hell, who am I to judge given how I've treated *every* woman I've bedded?

Despite my change in attitude, I've kept a watchful eye— minus the malice or resentment—on my parents, and I've witnessed Dad treat Mama like she's the most precious of jewels. He makes sure she takes her meds, visits the shrink— most times rearranging his schedule to go with her. And then there's Jace. I know what a "happy Jace" looks like but nothing comes close to this.

Is everything exactly as I want? I'm in the process of figuring that out. I *do* know there will always be a gaping hole in my life where Jimmy used to be, and seeing all the pieces of my family finally come together, I feel released of the responsibility I never should have had.

And now I can finally focus on me.

Chapter
THIRTY-THREE

Ragan

One Year Later

I GRAB MY CELL PHONE FROM THE EDGE OF THE DESK and press Accept. "Hello."

"I heard someone got their first private commission. Congratulations, sugar."

A wide smile spreads over my lips. I remember the first time he called me *sugar*. I hadn't wanted to admit it, but the smooth, sexiness of his voice elicited a rush of goosebumps, much like the ones that trail over my skin now.

"How did you know?" My pieces have been selling at an unbelievable rate. And now that I've been commissioned by a widely acclaimed TV celebrity, it's the talk of the art industry. There was even an article in *Fine Art Connoisseur Magazine* with the headline: "The New Face of Contemporary Art as Depicted by Ragan S. Prescott."

The girl who, over a year ago, couldn't afford a car repair

without handouts from others. Here I am now in New York, living a life I never would've dreamed of. And to boot, Andrés is partnering with me to open The Prescott Gallery next spring. Everything is happening so quickly that I barely have time to wonder if it really is the fairytale I thought didn't happen to girls like me.

"Maybe I'm keeping tabs on you," Branch replies.

"Hundreds of miles away and you still can't get me out of your head, huh?"

I hear his smile through the phone. "You'd like that, wouldn't you?"

Hell yeah, I would. He's already assumed permanent residence in my head, but I know he isn't in a place to hear that. And quite frankly I'm scared shitless to say it.

My assistant Erin shuts off the back office lights and heads toward the front with the rest of us.

I wish I had more time to talk to Branch. "Hey, thanks for calling and I hate to cut this call short, but I have to run. They're taking me out to celebrate."

"Don't tell me I'm missing a party," he jokes.

"Yup."

"Next time I'm there we'll have our own private celebration."

"Ragan, the Uber's here!" Kale shouts.

"I have to—"

"I know. I heard. Have a great time. You deserve it."

"Thanks, Branch."

I shove the phone in my bag and walk out into the night air. The city is bursting with a vibrancy and expectation that filters its way through our small group. I settle in the back of the luxury Uber, smiling at the elation of Andrés, Erin,

Autumn, and the other gallery staff. They chatter on and on about my big sale but all I think about is Branch and his promise of a private celebration, wondering what he meant, and thinking how much I'd prefer that to whatever this night may hold.

Chapter
THIRTY-FOUR

Ragan

I STEP OUT OF THE COFFEE SHOP AND SCAN THE BUSY street. New Yorkers hail cabs, slide into Ubers or walk in line with crowds of businessman, tourists and various assortments of others rushing along before they are trampled. After a sip of my latte, I join in with them, a wider smile spreading over my lips with each step.

Look at me. On my own in a city that would have gobbled me up and spit me out this time two years ago. I'm going to take New York by storm. I can feel it. I have it in me, it was *always* in me. It was just hidden behind the clutter of heartache and pain. I'd thought I was broken and down for the count, but I was never really broken, I was just a little bent. And thanks to Branch, I now see that it's okay to be that way. The key is to straighten yourself out as best you can and get back in the race.

Sometimes that doesn't happen. My mom was a prime example. And I, too, would have been an example. Ethan had been the final straw. He'd gotten in my head and he'd beaten me down and without even realizing it, I'd let him. But it wasn't just him.

My beatdown started the day I was born. The person who gave me life—she wasn't the nurturing mother I needed. That I deserved. And the person she passed me on to, Cassidy, she abused my body and my mind every day for over a decade. And then when Ethan finally came along, I thought I'd been saved, that he'd come to rescue me, that he was my knight in shining armor. But he was no knight. He was a dark cloud that sealed in the pain and humiliation I'd covered with makeup and smiles. He was the heavy burden of remorse and fear I'd carried around for years. He was that subtle poison to my soul that was my ultimate downfall. I shudder to think what would have become of me had I not encountered the one person who I didn't think would ever give a girl like me a second glance.

But he did.

Despite my pigheadedness. Despite my less-than-stellar attitude. He kept coming back for more. And somehow, it finally sank in. I'm someone who deserves to be loved and to give love. I have something to offer this world. I just couldn't see it before because of the negativity and darkness that surrounded and eventually claimed me as its own.

But this last year has been somewhat of a rebirth that I'll celebrate every year instead of the actual day I was born. It seems as if my life has finally aligned with the stars.

And a special treat with a cherry on top was finding out that the karma I'd been hoping for, really did exist. It finally showed up and served Cassidy her just deserts. Her new family didn't repeat *my* family's dreadful mistake of concealing the truth about the monster she is—they reported her abuse. And once all the skeletons began falling from her closet, Noah and I were contacted by the district attorney. We were allowed to submit video testimony regarding our history with Cassidy. I was relieved that it was admissible because I wasn't sure I could be in the same room with her without the risk of being arrested myself. I couldn't do that to CeeCee.

And the turn of events I still can't fathom…Dad testified against her as well. If he did it to redeem himself or as a start to healing a family that could never be healed, I don't know, but karma finally assumed possession on the wickedness that was Cassidy Merritt. If what I hear is true, the women in that prison will give her every bit of the sentence a child abuser deserves.

With all of that behind me, the future is all I see.

Sometimes you have to distance yourself from the past, even if it's the only life you know. And although Branch was the beacon in the midst of a blinding storm, I had to leave him behind, too. In order to be my best self, I had to get out of Blue Ridge.

My life in Georgia was the shit nightmares are made of. I don't know why I was given such a rough start, but now I firmly believe I had to walk that path for a reason. Maybe it happened because it now enables me to help others, or maybe it happened because it was the only way I could provide a voice for those who suffer as I once did…I don't know. But whatever the reason, this is my life. I'm embracing it and I'm ready to own it.

Chapter
THIRTY-FIVE

Ragan

Super Bowl Sunday

"SEE YOU GUYS AT *STANDINGS*," I REMIND AUTUMN, Erin, Kale, Andrés, and Jax about watching the Super Bowl at the East Village Sports Bar. "And remember to wear your Redhorns jerseys."

"Okay, okay, okay. Isn't this like your fourth time reminding us within the last hour?" Erin asks. "We'll be heading out as soon as we wrap up the final details for the curator."

Had I actually reminded them four times? Jeez. I must really have Branch on the brain. "Sounds great. Bye for now and thanks for everything today, guys."

Unless it's for a private showing, the gallery is typically closed on Sundays but we came in at the crack of dawn to arrange the newer selections for the curator tomorrow. It's kind of a huge deal so we needed all hands on deck if we wanted everything absolutely perfect for the meeting with

Jean Pierre.

I exit Andrés's gallery and step toward the exhibit windows, my eyes wide and a huge smile spreading over my lips as I move past each of the paintings displayed in the four windows. I stop at the last one and read the signage.

Contemporary Art
Evening Sale
Property from the Collection of Ragan S. Prescott

A jolt of excitement urges me to jump up and down like a kid who's just unwrapped the gift she's been hoping for all of her life.

"Eh, what the hell?" I let out a little yelp and then giggle to myself when the passersby react to my strange display. The enthusiasm is just too much to contain within one person.

I grab my phone and dial Noah.

"Hey, sis."

"Hi, little brother. Check this out." I press the button that flips the call to video and show Noah the paintings in the four windows.

"Holy shit, Ragan!"

I turn the screen to see my brother's face. "I know, right!"

"Have I told you lately how proud I am of you?"

"Yeah. About a hundred times. But you can tell me again," I add with a giggle.

"I'm so proud of you I can hardly stand it."

"Thank you, Noah. So what's happening with the move?"

"Grey and I are still on schedule to be there within the next two weeks. Just tying up some loose ends here, then we're headed your way."

"Awesome. I'm so excited. We're finally going to be to-gether again."

"After all this time."

"And after all we've been through," I reply, my voice wistful.

"Yeah, who would have predicted that two kids who had such fucked-up beginnings would have the lives we have now? Hugely successful and finally happy. The only thing left is snagging a husband for you."

"I'm not ready for anything like that. I've told you that like a billion times already."

"Yeah, because you're still holding out hope for *The Man on Fire*," he air quotes.

"Shut up, Noah. Am not."

"Are too. Every single time you mention that guy's name your voice goes all dreamy. I'll admit he's hot as hell but play-ers like him don't settle down, Ragan."

A *player* wouldn't have done all the things Branch has done for me. Would he? "Noah, just hush and keep packing. My Uber's here. Tell Greyson I said hello and I can't wait to see him."

"I'll just bet you can't, *stalker*. Stay away from his Instagram."

"He shouldn't be so pretty."

"Am I going to have to fight you for *my* man?"

"Maybe. Or at least share him until I find one of my own."

"Once we get the gallery going, our next line of business is getting you laid."

"You are the silliest thing. Bye, Noah."

He lets out a chuckle. "Love you."

"Love you, too."

I'm the first to arrive at *Standings*…no surprise there. I glance toward the bar and catch the eye of my favorite bartender Brinkley, and she gestures for me to grab the booth that's been secretly reserved for us. By *reserved*, I mean, Brinkley asked a group of her friends to occupy the space until I could get here. I slip her the normal *reservation fee* and order beers for the seven of us. I figure the beers will arrive around the same time as my straggling workmates.

The excitement for the game penetrates every molecule of air in the bar. Scanning the crowd of sports fans, I smile at the flurry of red, gray, and white caps, the shirts, hoodies and jerseys. Mine boasts Branch's number—ten.

The table nearest me is a rowdy group of guys, and they're going on and on about who'll win. I didn't wager on the outcome of the game, but if I had, all my money would be on the Redhorns.

I'm so giddy about seeing Branch—even if it's just on television. We've stayed in touch to a certain degree. Well…sort of. It's been a text here or there and a few short phone calls but that's about it. I haven't seen him face-to-face since the day I said goodbye…just as I suspected I wouldn't. So me being me, I've tried to catch all of his TV appearances as well as any magazines and online articles that I can find. Hmm. Maybe Noah's right…I *am* a stalker.

About twenty minutes pass before my work crew comes strolling toward the booth, all wearing their Redhorns jerseys.

I grin at them. "Guess those four reminders paid off. You guys look great. Could totally pass for *real* football fans."

"What makes you think we aren't?" Jax asks.

"You and Andrés, sure. But Erin, Autumn, and Kale…no way."

"Your beers," Brinkley says stepping up to the booth with a tray. "The chips, queso, and hot wings are on the house," she adds as she places everything on the table then slides in beside me.

I take in her change of clothes and smile. "You're wearing your Redhorns jersey! Yay! And thanks for holding the booth," I shout over the noise.

"I had to extend my shift to get away with it this time, but no biggie."

Brinkley was one of the first people I met outside of the gallery staff when I first moved here. Andrés and his wife Eva absolutely adore CeeCee, so from time to time, they take her for overnights which gives me time to explore the city. And sometimes, I simply want to do that alone.

I'd wandered into *Standings* one evening when a Redhorns game was on. Brinkley was working the bar that night, and in typical bartender fashion she got me talking about what ailed me. As we watched the game, she mentioned how hot Branch was and when she noticed my reaction, that was all it took. I gabbed on and on about growing up in the same town with him. Soon after that night, she fast became my New York version of Hayley, only much less weird.

It's crazy loud in the bar. Mix that with liquor, and it's bound to get even louder. When everyone within my proximity begins tossing out their fantasy football picks, I tune out their voices and strain to hear the guys behind me debate the hype that surrounds Branch McGuire. I inwardly smile, thinking how amazing it feels to have intimate knowledge about the guy who others perceive as larger than life. To know the man behind the jersey—yeah, it's pretty freaking awesome.

After a hilarious *Doritos* commercial, the opening ceremony begins with the commentators discussing the starting lineup. And it all begins with Branch McGuire. With so much noise, I only catch bits and pieces from the sports correspondent.

…one of the top quarterbacks in the country, first in the nation in completion percentage.

Oh, God. I wish they'd pipe it down. And then as if they all heard my inward cry, the noise levels out just enough and I focus on the next sportscaster.

Not only does he have sensational throws, but he's been doing it with his legs throughout the season as well, which has added another dimension to the Dallas offense.

He's earned the coaches respect and confidence that they can call any play anywhere on the field.

After brief player intros, they proceed to the coin toss, then the game starts. Both teams hold their own for the first three quarters. Contradictory to what's been floating around the last couple of weeks, it's a tight game. Not at all what was predicted, and the camera flashes to Branch more than it does any other player. He looks irritated. And he's caught reprimanding his teammates on more than one occasion.

During the next commercial, Brinkley and I rush to the ladies room. Luckily, we get to skip the lines and head for the employee facilities. When she lingers in the mirror to freshen her makeup, I rush her out of the bathroom, only giving her time to reapply her rouge red lipstick. She puts up a fuss but I explain we don't have time for anything else. I grab her hand, tugging her behind me as she teases me about my fascination with Branch. And unlike Ragan of the past, I don't deny it. We've even planned to attend a few of his games next season. Of course, I'll have to add Hayley to the mix. She and Brinkley have become the sisters I never had.

We slide into our seats just as the screen flips back to the game. It's down to the last quarter, the last few minutes and very well the last play of the night.

Dallas has the ball.

The hike is called.

Branch takes a few steps back, looks to his left and with a pat on the ball, he sends it soaring down the field just before a mass of green and yellow pile atop him. But they were too late. Number eight caught the ball on the ten yard line and ran the play to completion, earning the Redhorns the Super Bowl win! The bar erupts in cheers, mine amongst the loudest. The camera zooms in on Branch and my heart skips a beat. He's winded, he's sweaty, and he's gorgeous. And once again, he's proven why he's *The Man on Fire*.

Chapter
THIRTY-SIX

Ragan

The Day After The Super Bowl

AFTER A PROSPEROUS MORNING WITH JEAN PIERRE, I call it quits and gleefully head off to run my errand. I've decided to start a new project today. The idea actually came to me after watching the Super Bowl. As Branch's stats and various slow motion shots continuously flashed across the screen yesterday, they inspired me to paint a montage of images…all of him.

Standing in the magazine section of the local bookstore, I thumb through a few pages of *Sports Illustrated* until I come to a section highlighting Branch and expel a gasp. *Holy shit!* He's naked. He's fully *naked*. I horn in on every angle of the picture and slowly exhale the air I didn't realize I'd been holding, unable to tear my eyes away from those rippling biceps or the thick band of muscles that define his thighs. *Sweet baby Jesus.* This man is the purest definition of sin.

And his pose—bloody brilliant. He's standing with a slight twist of his torso. His long fingers curve over a football that he holds just below his waist in a position that conceals his goodies. I'm certain every woman, and quite a few men, are more than a little disappointed by the placement of that ball.

I exhale a wistful sigh. *This* is the man I had the pleasure of seeing up close and personal. The man who ate my pussy like he was being paid, fucked me past the point of delirium, then sent me on my way the next day. The man I'm still hung up on and shouldn't be.

He appears untouchable. A magnificent specimen gracing a two-page spread. I can just imagine the photo shoot. Despite the softer side of Branch McGuire, he's an arrogant ass most times. I'm sure he was ogled by everyone on the set, and I'm equally sure he was still every bit the full-of-himself package of man candy he always is. Totally unaffected by the lingering eyes of those behind the lens.

I smooth my finger across the image of a man I'd gotten to know, a man I can now claim as my friend. An asshat with an unshakeable disposition that I'd often found to be a turnoff when he was taunting me, but I'd be lying if I'd said it wasn't just as much of a turn-on.

The rustle of customers pulls me from my deliciously dirty thoughts and I proceed to grab every publication I can find that features Branch on the cover. After I'm certain I've secured all they have, I head to the register. The cashier glances at the stack of magazines, deep lines forming between her barely there eyebrows when she looks up at me. She probably thinks I'm some kind of psycho stalker. I can see how it may appear that way. I grin at her and slide my credit card into the reader.

Back at home, I grab a bottle of wine, get CeeCee situated, then in no time at all, I'm immersed in my project. Inspired by my muse, I find myself soon lost in what I'm doing. Occasionally I look over at Cecelia as she mimics Mommy. At the small table beside me, she's drawing a picture of her stuffed animals. I take a sip of wine and decide on a flat-white base, lightly brushing it over the canvas when the doorbell rings.

"I'll be right back, sweetie," I say to CeeCee and wonder who would be dropping by in the middle of the afternoon. After one last sip of wine, I place the empty glass on the counter, then cross the room. When I press the button for the door cam, I damn near lose every ounce of that Chardonnay when I see intense blue eyes staring back at me. *Oh my God!* It's *him.* The one man I never expected to see anywhere besides on a TV screen. The man responsible for the amazing changes in the lives of me and my daughter. And he's standing on the other side of my door. A flicker of excitement sparks in my chest as my insides turn to mush. Not bothering to check my appearance, I reach for the knob to remove the barrier between us.

"Hey," he says, and flashes that stomach-flipping, breathtaking smile.

Oh holy hell. How can one simple word turn my knees turn to Jell-O? I lean against the door for support. "Hey."

An awkward expression shifts his features.

"What are you doing here? I mean...I kinda thought it would be much longer before I...before we...I thought you said I was ready to stand on my own."

"You have a little something right here." Branch touches a

hand to my cheek, his fingers working to wipe away the paint smudges. "And I said you can stand on your own because it's true."

"Then I don't understand. Why are you here?" Not that I'm complaining, but it's been over a year and I'm so caught off guard that I can barely breathe, let alone form coherent thought. I part my lips and remind myself to speak, but the words are stuck in my throat, so I don't bother. Instead I take him in. The dark blond hair cropped short, the thick brows that hood dazzling blue eyes, the prominent jawline, the pink lips…oh those full, pink, fuck-me lips. *Good God, he's nice to look at.* Or in my case, gawk at like a raving lunatic.

As my gaze remains fixed on those perfect lips, he steps over the threshold, and his large strong hands frame my face. With my body frozen in place and my heartbeat stammering in my ears, I lift my eyes to his and I swear a part of my soul drifts into him.

He's going to kiss me. Branch McGuire is going to kiss me.

He lowers his head and brushes his mouth ever so softly over mine, meeting my lips with a light touch. On instinct my body curls into him and a piece of his soul, equal in part to what I'd given him, breathes new life into me. My mouth molds to his in an inexplicable rightness that answers the question his words didn't.

This kiss is everything. It awakens the dormant part of my existence. It assures me that I'm not in this alone and that I never will be again. His tongue slips inside my mouth tasting of me as I tenderly do the same of him. And in this moment, I feel my heart heal completely.

He draws me closer and I let go of everything except him. Except now. Except the irreversible pairing of two beacons that through time and space emerge as salvaged hearts that have miraculously survived a storm of chaos and heartache.

My life has been a shroud of impenetrable obscurity punctuated by moments of clarity. And this kiss is precisely that. Nothing has ever been as clear, as certain, as this. It redefines life as I know it and it buries the shattered beginnings of my past.

The kiss lasts for several long minutes until Branch eventually pulls away, slightly winded and his eyes soft with a tenderness that melts every piece of my heart.

If that earth-shattering kiss hadn't conveyed the depth of his feelings, the warmth of his gaze confirms everything I could ever hope for, but I need to hear him say the words. "So...are you going to answer me now? Why is Branch McGuire on my doorstep?"

He shakes his head and exhales a long sigh, smiling to himself, almost as if he can't believe what he's about to say. "Because you're that girl I can't stop thinking about."

THE END

Coming Soon

Dancing In The Dark
An Untouched Series Spinoff

A SNIPPET FROM
DANCING IN THE DARK

Allison

N O MORE GOING BACK AND FORTH—LIVING IN Chicago to appease my parents but longing for the freedom that New York City provides. Today makes it official. I'd finally cut the strings…sort of. I mean, I can't very well live without Daddy's credit cards, not yet anyway.

Upper East Side Manhattan is the place I now call home. My mail has been forwarded, my clothing has filled every available space in the two guest room closets, I'm back with my ballet company and I'm knee deep in plans for a spectacular splash that will properly welcome me to the New York scene. The only thing left to do is break the news to my family—especially my big overbearing brother Aiden—that I'm not living alone, that I actually moved in with my boyfriend William Holt.

That conversation won't go over very well, which is the only reason I've put it off. That…plus Daddy may cut me off if he realizes I'm living in a manner he deems inappropriate for his little girl. Yes, I'm an adult in every sense of the word, but he doesn't quite see it that way. At least not yet. And with just one word from Aiden, Daddy will end all discussion of my 'needs' and cancel any access I have to the family fortune. So until I find a way to make money of my own, my living arrangement must remain a secret. Thing is…what can I do that will provide the same lifestyle the Raine billions have afforded me since birth?

STAY CONNECTED WITH LILLY

Facebook Fan Page
www.facebook.com/authorlillywilde

Facebook Reader Group
www.facebook.com/groups/TheWildeLillies

Instagram
www.instagram.com/authorlillywilde

Twitter
twitter.com/authorlilly

Goodreads
www.goodreads.com/author/show/8577407.Lilly_Wilde

Google+
plus.google.com/115013089578343874604

LinkedIn
www.linkedin.com/in/lillywilde

YouTube
www.youtube.com/channel/UCyzbRGz2o-pIRMDq0ncw3Jw

Pinterest
www.pinterest.com/lillywilde

Thank you for reading *Salvaged Hearts*. If you enjoyed it, I would love to hear from you! Please take a moment to leave a review at your favorite retailer.
Thanks!

Would you like to be a part of Lilly's upcoming book releases? Sign up to be a member of her launch team.

ABOUT THE AUTHOR

Lilly Wilde is the Author of The Untouched Series (Untouched, Touched, Touched By Him, Only His Touch and Forever Touched). She is a wife and mom who loves to fill each day with happiness and laughter. Lilly loves to dream, get lost in fantasy and create alternate worlds in which we can escape ever so often. She's down-to-earth, engaging and compassionate with a great sense of humor. Her laughter is one of the first qualities that you'll notice; you'll become instantly drawn to her witty and fun-loving spirit.

Lilly spent a lot of time daydreaming as a child which led to numerous hours of reading and eventually the writing of poetry. The first story Lilly began writing was entitled He Lied To Me, a novel she plans to complete in the near future. After years of starting and stopping several novels, she eventually set a goal to complete her debut novel, Untouched.

Her stories are of strength, growth, facing demons and stepping outside your comfort zone. They often surround topics of family and love and the beauty of both.

45039497R00138

Made in the USA
Columbia, SC
21 December 2018